AS I TRUDGE THROUGH THE VALLEY

by

Brian P Matheny

ISBN: 9798447054359

1.

As I trudge through the valley, the dread of another morning encircles me. Nothing left. A feeble allegiance breaches my ever-present remoteness, that giant space between life's petrifying grip and the subdued specter's isolation. Who has not suffered sincerely? Who has not hurtled themselves toward something remarkably ill-defined? Though concord is present, I exist in a vacuum of preposterous trivialities. I recall things spoken by well-wishers tossing dirt upon the graves of those recently departed. A man of shrouded depravity coveting those sensibilities coiled in the stomach of sorrow to appreciate what has eluded me since the doleful day I entered this world.

The systems of thought I rely upon to govern my motives, whether they be of a good or evil nature, revolve around the same dying sun. The factious sky is always moving, always shifting from day into night and from the hunger of a child's mouth to the stuffed stomach of a vanishing old man. Clemency lurks between the world of innocence and the world of servants satiated on humility and sin and guilt and remorse, lives lived beyond all explanation. A man full of crippling expectations transforms himself into nails hammered down by later disappointments. Failure is a brutish guide who leads with eyes burnt and ears pulsing with tar and wax.

My wretched nerves are like coiled barbed wire stretched tight, and tomorrow seems like a prolonged bereavement. It is still early morning, yet I sense uneasiness slithering under my skin. The lingering dread gyrates around me in a hushed state of unraveling agony. Awkwardly coddling the blankness within, insincerity fails me as another new day flops stillborn to the unkempt floor.

I wonder if they know? I wonder if this same voice speaking now will be there when tomorrow's gloom is but a crack in the veneer of years forgotten? What could possibly make this sensation of unending unselfishness end? Was it the manner in which I have lived life so carelessly and unrepentant? No sense dwelling on it now.

What is coming is coming. I am but a wistful mirror of tragedy, a revolting reflection of the fleeting optimism I once clung to as an immature man. A price paid for the mendacious manufacturing of a world without friends or enemies. The ever- present truthfulness of my situation is barely visible like a musty shadow hung in the room no one enters. Can this unbearable smell get any worse?

I hesitantly recall the day I began undergoing sensations of the sickly something inside. It was just a brief glimpse of the gnawing contentment mankind so veraciously thrives after as the hours tumble and the glasses run dry. It made me wrench at first. The wretchedness soiling my stomach morphed into a slight glimmer while sluggishly perfecting its presentation. A way to exhume myself from this tumbling mental anguish. A way to avoid looking down the mouth of hubris and confinement unbecoming. I should attempt to procure something dignified, something brutally honest. I am paralyzed figuratively without exception. I should address my uncertainties and tell all those who might listen how little I think of myself. I should do a lot of awful things to let someone inside of my head. We all should. And the appalling fact that a majority of this anemic society do not provides me with all the ripe indulgences I will ever require. Barely require.

Where shall I dare to begin? It was one day in a long series of tedious days in November when the car struck the light pole and moved no more. Neither did I.

Ambition, for some, is a strange and unwelcomed bedfellow. It is calculating, vague and surreptitiously drenched in deep-rooted perspiration. I envisioned myself as someone who would someday write the next pulverizing prodigious novel. The contemporaneous next "Tom Sawyer" or "On the Road" would tumble from timid fingers typing.

After spending a lifetime habitually falling, inevitably, I foresaw an instance when I would tumble hard and crack open my skull on some dimly lit pavement. The yoke of all those rustic literary visions swirling around in my head would spill out leaving only the blood stains and birth pangs of a tragic American miscreant splattered across brittle pages. My forefathers were all unabated ghosts. I can barely communicate the soul devouring sadness required these days to pass for a living breathing consciousness swaying over the wounded landscapes dotting this county's run down and depreciating town halls. Homes, abounded in ethnic plurality, once stretched across this miserable downtrodden earth with lights in their windows and entertained faces unaware of the coming taste of autumn.

I can still remember the boy I was, pressing my nose against the frigid windows of our trailer home looking into the boundless goodnight. So long ago. Sometimes, though, not long enough.

One bitter February morning in my youth, I awoke to find my mother's new boyfriend shivering next to my bed with a rugged drugged look in his eyes. Barren of purpose. In a voice, I will hopefully never misplace, he said, "the only ones who survive this wretched pool of leeches are the ones who live with the coldest of blood. That way, the blood suckers won't find you appetizing and leave you alone." He was truly unimaginative and unadorned, but he could not have been more correct in his assessment regarding the fragility of life.

So many times I have paused to allow the moss of life its due. And so many more times have I marvelously relented in the face of pending doom. This defect in my character makes me question the very fabric of my memories. If so many things could possibly go erroneous in the life of one man, how could mankind imagine serenity or sanity or a time when the unquenchable finally becomes drenched in libations?

It's hard to appreciate the mind of a man who describes himself as being a period mark, as the proverbial end of a sentence behind an antiquated dictionary full of words assembled into one long run-on sentence stretching out toward a time when time was not mentioned. It is here that one's fathomable future appears enigmatic. The quintessential void.

There is something mystical and maddening regarding finality. Something about being a punctuated placement. In a sequence of meanderings without meanings, those who deny the very foundation necessary to perceive a beginning without an end are truly lost. It was here I reluctantly met myself. At the end of the very beginning.

The roaring laughter of life all seemed so harmless when that particular day started. I was still mind-numb and dimly reeling from all the intoxicates I had heavily, and thoroughly, consumed the prior evening. Waves of vague pre-blackout glimpses lapped against me like the sensation of being licked by a repugnant coated thorny tongue, a tongue pulsing with infection, with blood blisters, lapping up the drunken evening's demise.

I struggled to accurately align my many misguided intentions preceding the alcohol-induced elation, the fruition of one's spirit on spirits upon awakening, but all clarity was stillborn. The dreadful realization came to me quickly. I was not born that morning into the hearth of reassuring bed sheets, but instead, was scrumptiously situated in a blackout jail cell, godless and gray.

A sulking sudden movement of the mind arrives when it detects the scent and surface of those jail plastic bed mats swallowing one's face covered in saliva. This realization should not be underestimated nor unappreciated. I was sprawled out on the mat in half-soaking wet clothing smelling of the putrid pungent odor of urine mixed with madness.

What had I done again? The answer does not come all at once. Those memories couched within blackouts are like clouds in a burning sky filled with holes reaching into the infinite unease.

I remember the sirens, the police cars chasing me, then periods of escape followed by brief glimpses of the trailing acrimony. The sensation of cold air rushing into the windows as music pounded against my head. There was a deafening mix of thrill, of being chased and the resounding wail of Bob Dylan's rainy day dreams. I recall the silence followed by the feeling of being weightless as the car became airborne, then the dull crack of the pole. Airbag deployed.

All-consuming wafts of burning oil smoldering. Gas stench saturating. Smoke-filled lungs collapsing. Eyes crippled from the noxious fumes tearing. The cop's roaring car lights approached in the ever-present distance. I remember standing against the side of my once moving vehicle. Standing next to the crumbled and tainted, a temperate immobility washed over me. It was the knowing of moments such as this, moments of astute self-reflection, that unfounded knowledge that your life was going to veer off the path in a direction you could never have imagined nor chosen. I began to imagine my life happening in hindsight as the fleeting seconds of sanity fell from my shoulders like tiny midnight snowflakes descending onto an all too familiar desert.

Then came the shouting. Police, like ants, swarmed with guns drawn while I wavered wearing a drunken clown smile. "Get the fuck on the ground."

Knees jettisoned into my neck. The cuffs tightened around my twisted wrists as concord was not yet shattered. The officers were sullenly unamused with my antics. They did not care to even ask what was wrong with me. What kind of a person would, though, so thoughtlessly place his life, and the lives of others traveling the dark highway to destinations never fully understood, in such unnecessary danger?

Who would give up so much of their pretend freedoms bestowed upon them by an all-consuming, crumbling world of unhealthy and sedentary consumers to bear witness to authority bemoan in long futile gasps? The scrumptious sound arbitrators of judgment exhale when their system of control is challenged? Pathetic and feeble babbles. The goading gaggles cower when being pushed on by one not playing by the antiquated rules, those hideous dictates carved onto the bellies of madmen and warriors alike as their decomposing bodies wash upon the shores of disenchantment ad infinitum.

My belly boiled and churned with anticipation awaiting the law man's sanctions. The thought of losing everything to gain the world. The emptiness gained whilst giving it all away. Swaying minute by minute. In the drudges, life is coughed up and swallowed like the mama bird regurgitating the early worms into the beaks of her helpless chicks.

Time shudders and moves like glue, muddy and unfashionable, yet potential in its adhesive quality. Pondering over and over contextualized ambiguity, I cannot coherently invoke an honest thought regarding that doleful day I was born. I can barely remember my fragile appearance smoldering and covered in fragmented window shards as the car simmered loudly in its crushed finality. A moment of reflection paused my trembling. I considered whether I had become an enemy to the social fabric of those sufficient home owners feasting aimlessly up and down the trough?

The officers swore within inches of my face. They called me a bastard, a fake, a low life form unworthy to even lose the preciousness their security system provided. I was the deplorable guest who soiled the bed sheets before leaving.

"You've put our lives in danger chasing you, you piece of day-old bread scum. We could have died and never returned to our wives, our children, our mortgages and the luxurious lies we rely upon. You could have mattered like thick batter. You could have been fortified on the fearfulness we protect. You could have had a dog at your feet and a job affording you the privilege of driving a stake into the back of your head," said the sanguine law enforcer.

They were just getting warmed up with their innuendos designed to break my spirit. Unfortunately, I have no spirit left to break. Nothing worth breaking. Nothing distinguishable in the first place. All the stunned faces of authority cowered at my reluctance to bow to their serpent life diseases. I had planted myself in the figurative shoes of an unrelenting smog billowing as a staggering rate of moths swirled in unison toward the fawning moon, like motorized balloons bending the light fandango.

Things begin, always and inevitably, like the flawless resonance a cell door makes when closing behind and the untenable mark it leaves on the memory. A hoarfrost of stillness shelters the scattering and incarcerated mind as it settles into the suffocating air bleached with odors only found in jail. I was heavily intoxicated upon entering the police station. Waking was a blur.

The mocking mind drifts without direction across sorrow filled thoughts of time and space existing in one tangled and

taunt bite sized piece to torment. I refrained from deliberations over trivial tomorrows and things once done out of
gratitude or spite. Silvery things, those vile heirlooms of a
vulgar vocabulary, took a backseat to the present misfortune. A
sullen repentance tinged with spineless ambiguity would not
suffice.

Yet, there was still a hint of freedom most could or would
not value, but it is a freedom in the noblest, yet loftiest, sense
of the word. When gloom filled predictions and lamentations
regarding the approaching future unraveling are disrobed and
tattered, the encroaching senility of the jail cell becomes a
holy site where unrequited prayers for release bounce chaotically around. The listless prayers are forced to feed off the
denials mankind has put in motion.

The institutionally restrained are caged like abandoned
animals wallowing in wanton volition. The way forward. The
distance between one's face and the tiny cell window. Somber
eyes studying the parade of criminal entities processed as they
pass through authority's revolving door of misfortune. Even
though I was newly nestled behind the cell's window, those
uninitiated members dragged into the booking area appeared
sullen and infected with disbelief, but it won't take them long
to regurgitate the sickness swelling within. Soon they will
vomit all over in tiny exhales of regret.

Through the mental halos of alcoholic smog billowing in
my brain, I recalled having done something so undefinable, so
erroneous, yet I could not contain my blind admiration for
having done it. Some people live their entire lives being
dragged around from moment to moment, never realizing how
little they matter until the clang of a cold cell door slamming
awakens this enlightened fear of being caught. The incarcerated hours become hollow mouths. Each second scorching
the nerves. Becoming vague. An outpouring of anger initially
overtakes the mind of a contained man. Anger for not getting

away. Anger for not having made a true and unblemished escape from authority's claws long as tentacles across the oil-thick world. The corrupt and contaminated masses huddle under a veneer of fear these social approved harbingers of civility concoct to maintain a decency of their choosing. Those dealing in confinement turn living things into dead puddles of piss to waddle in. A flourishing consciousness unhampered by consequences has no home in here.

If I could only have driven faster and not lost control. If only I were divine, I never would have swung the car into that light pole ending my drunk addled parade of vindictiveness. But all things end. Even endings end. I recall thinking of leaving that dreadful cell someday. It would be a righteous day. The day I heave my blackened chest toward the gods of consequence and scream, "See me now you wretched pilots of demise. It is my turn to take the controls and drive this damn plane into the nearest mountain range."

I watched as the strung-out bodies of self-abused men, so recently ripped from great American streets and decaying abandoned homes, were brought into the jail. The alcohol-laced adrenaline my loathing soul had been feeding from began to draw down its charm, and I became sand-filled with remorse and indignity. The effects of the alcohol wore off like a frown becoming a face. Eyes blistering. Legs trembling.

My hands swelled and were weighed down, dropping as if to touch the floor before it swallowed me. The elusive exclusionary anticipation of a swift release from custody was long gone, and behind me was nothing but endless roads of what could, should, or might have been. Soon, the guards forgot about the self-appointed lump of decay lying prone in the cell. They did not even notice I turned into oblique stone. They mistook me for the concrete floor and walked upon my cold soaked head as they mopped the urine spilt from the floundering animal man.

I wandered off into a fitful of less than allusive memories. Not knowing if they were turning over in my mind or if it was I turning them over, haphazardly, I waited patiently for a somber speculation to tug me from my emptiness. I disingenuously altered the time sequence of the prior evening's events in my mind. One must shroud themselves in plausible denials when those sorceress sensations of guilt and regret seek to overcame.

"It was not me, Officer. I was withering. I was under the car hanging on for dear life. The monster was in the driver's seat beating out time with callouses on his feet. Beating out the rhythm of a misspent juvenescence, I filled evenings wishing I was in someone else's daydreams or midnight rendezvous where neighbor girls were slick and willing. Can you hear me, Officer? I am bursting wide with illicit vibrations. Moans and groans. Ancient sounds shuddering. My godless hole within coughs up the vacant. And the subtle wails brought forth should not be mistook for empty belches belched during one's sanctified return to ambiguity. Can you deny me this, Officer?"

The silence was comical. I smiled before falling into a cacophony of frightful tomorrows covered in a blanket of wool worn yesterdays. I slept like one dragging the dead within.

The next morning came over me like a rifle blast to the face, buckshot scattering the suddenness of wakening. Every blood cell morphed into a swarm of frantic fire ants all scurrying toward a darkened hole, seeking the nurturing decorum of a mighty queen now deceased. I did not want to open my eyes.

I was unwilling to acknowledge gnarled verisimilitudes, those drunken impersonators from prior evenings coddling misfortune's maleficence. But the smell of the jail cell intervened. Reality overcame my flagrant attempt at self-deception. The deep throated monstrosities of fate gathered around like dark angles scoffing and feeding off the vile bile of innocence pouring from slit wrists. With bandaged fingers, I scraped thickened crust from my eyes and peeled back my eyelids. The stench of urine-soaked clothes smothered me with impurities. The pungent scent of rubber tires, exhaust smoke and gasoline mixed with the familiar alcohol saturated liquid one's liver expels.

Was I still convinced of my being at that point? I mean, I was at a loss for even putting into context what the next seconds would entail, let alone the day and the aborted days thereafter. A moment when the simple surrendering to one's unflinching character arises and dies all within the same breath? The heedless hour baptizes not with fire nor flood. Instead, it rids one of wanton dignity with gore, rotten as an apple's core covered in moss and left discarded in a field of smoldering coal.

I am not a specter of my own misfortune, but a willing and sometimes numb character of its construction, of its conclusions. The box I found myself in was not created from the hands of men. The brick wall grayness was birthed from my futile allegiance to societal norms devoid of flavor.

This was of my doing. My misplaced being in the world. The insincere cell walls reflect nothing that was not already residing within. The tiny window of the drunk tank was not a window to look out of, but one to look into.

The guards walked in front of my shivering solitude without paying any mind to the internal struggle I was enduring. They were not the least bit interested in what I had become or how far down the precipice I had fallen. To them, I was merely an absence on a morbid crumbling stage of fading mores. The unfortunate backdrop of a play performed by delinquents trumpeting towering misfortunes so carelessly.

I was a leech on a beach. Dissecting the slow passing and arriving acceptance of my gnawing situation, salty and blistering. The thought of being locked away from community standards and eloquent foundations was met with a subtle elation. There would be no mistaking it. Caged was I.

All I have known or would know, the self I was aware of and its shadow, the nothingness, and the hopeless daring to become, were throbbing behind my forehead, waiting to be stillborn. I was not a man of untold humility, but an unsettled criminal in the seething and judging eyes of jurisprudence. The luminous sympathy granted to those of a benevolent nature, those not afraid to bare themselves on the altar of self-abasement, was not afforded nor ushered to me.

I was not whisked away from captivity in a fleeting reprieve. I was left jail-cell humbled. Left to wander about in drunkenly inept thinking. The givers of forgiveness left me nothing more than dirty needles to dabble in and gauze to dab the blood drippings. A coal blackened mark was placed on my forehead by the sinister priests of prison immortality to ward off any novice naysayers looking for excuses. I was all etched up like a charcoal etching perversity.

My cage slowly slipped into the forever forgotten desig-nation amongst the growing abandoned hues filling the already packed jail. After much time prostrating before the appalling future, the door clanked with the sound of a key forcing open the lock. There was a vacuum-like sound as the door sucked opened, as if I was being slurped into a novel yet deeper level of Hades.

I first saw the outstretched arm bathed in blue before noticing the guard's face. The guard was stern and unresponsive to emotions, something I doubted was for my benefit alone. His quizzical facial features appeared to have been cultivated meticulously through years spent riddled by internal ambivalence. Some men were given to wantonness while others were given to the forbearing taste of grief. This man was given to neither. His eyes were inclined visitants scrutinizing a thousand dead seashores covered with the dying calm of driftwood decomposing.

"Get up, it's time to get booked."

And just like that, the realization that I was no longer the Moirai of my own marionette existence became hauntingly present. A pale puppet contorted from the pulling of many tangled and twisted knots. Strings with intention, with tension, with rules governing were applied with infected fish hooks to all involuntary muscular movements.

The guard morphed into a gangling conductor with eight giant arms and swore vigorously as he refused to play the sorrowful song of self-repentance. Without a fraction of self-reliance, my will bent to his every command. Like a half-eaten, half-beaten dog at his master's smoldering feet, I obeyed beyond comprehension. This I found immediately gratifying.

"Get undressed and stand against the wall. You're going to be showered and deloused before entering the holding area. You will then wait to be called before the judger. Depending on the judger's orders, you will be placed in a cell to wait. Do you understand?"

"Yes." It was all my throbbing mouth was able to muster. "Yes." I waited for what I did not know. Waiting can be a blessing if you find yourself tumbling wastefully down the septic shaft of uncertainty, a shaft birthing no bottom, no inane familiarity. Tumbling into a palpitating pit populated with burnt embers floating. Never knowing the ghastly foundation of finality residing at the bottom allows the often conscientious person to reconsider their willingness to be moral in the face of certain authority. A tormented plunge without the cathartic thud. I waited for each and every decree the guard uttered. "Yes."

As the guard turned his back toward me, in a softer than air whisper, I felt these words pass painfully over my lips, "I will follow your orders with an eyeless disregard for each and every mandate, and I will do so wearing the grin of insincerity. You see, I am fake fumes. I am not to be trusted with compassionate gestures. Do not, for one moment, think I will arise at some future juncture to fracture the bread, that moldy loaf overrun with airless vernacular fungi, with you or your devious flatterers. Yes. You must see. I have always waited. But I am now at home, for home is where you are the most unhappy." The guard did not notice my whispered words as we walked.

The guard's hideous momentum continued as he led me from the delousing chamber and steered me straight into the booking area. The headless guard stood over me like a glorious halo waiting to hand out the kind of persecution only the shivering seraphs could truly understand. Redemption was not the road I trudged.

The thought of potentially waking from this emasculated imbroglio to find it was all a livid aberration, a humbling nightmare like hallucination, was not in the least bit consoling nor did it provide me a temporary reprieve from the here nor the hereafter. Life becomes all misty opaque when awakened from its dreadful reverie. Groundless convictions opiate no more. To find oneself roused in a convincing world compounded by demonic delusions of grandeur and the remote hissing sounds of regrets regurgitating was the plight of the modern man. The feigning of forgetfulness no longer permits imperishable things entrance into the mind of a confined man unhinged. The glorious beasts who once dined on the affections, aspirations, and warmth of the civilized, inevitably starved to death on the edge of another forgotten era.

I stood patiently in the booking area while long dormant and buried emotions shredded me with their hollowed out sobering intensity. I was the numb falcon losing sight of the falconer. I circled farther and farther out into the fog of dubiousness. The trembling ascendancy of the falconer's arm with its metaphoric grip on sanity, its wistful call beckoning for a return to home, and its glaring command to find a stable place to land were all but usurped by the guard's penitentiary demands.

I was under the delusion that I was a thinking disease unraveling. I considered my rolling self-contentment as something deserving of a throne perched high above the needs of others kneeling before their unfortunate lots. To be an authentic self befitting the title, "Sacred Sacrifice," was not something I was immune to theoretically, but when you have nothing of importance dwelling within you, it is both pointless and absurd to sacrifice your utter emptiness.

I was like the didactic dog relinquishing his bone before returning home alone. For the betterment of affluent sufferers, those headstrong consumers nestled atop piles of earthly indulgences, I squandered ripened and sympathetic ways over the last several years. They slowly slithered from the menacing mortal coils impeding my cadaverous movements somewhere either up or down the sickly path I trudged.

Rummaging through the trash heap of time for a more prosperous and consequential state of discernment, one not subsumed by the crumbling decor of modern indecency, I somehow tumbled through prior albatross encounters unscathed, but no more would I be unburdened. None of the guards questioned my silence. I stood pensively. Rumpus thoughts drifted off while staring into the fake wood veneer of the booking desk. What if they mistook my lack of concern for procedures as a sign of guilt. Guilt and mute being old bedfellows.

Finally, the gofer guard behind the desk asked in a stern voice if I was aware of the charges being leveled against me. He made a point of asking me twice. I nodded in the affirmative, then a wee drip of urine dripped below. A sign of the surrendered.

The guard told me to stand against the wall. I was to be photographed, then fingerprinted. I was tempted to ask him for a slight favor, to be let go with a warning or something to ease my way from this frigid place. I was then ushered emphatically back into the tiny holding cell from which I came. The listless guard slammed the door in my face. Alone in my cell, I drew inward and cowered in the corner fretting tomorrow's return. My inward place was constructed from the same staunch marble of antiquity used to fashion the sturdy walls of philosophic halls where heroic Greek orators pondered over essence, aesthetics, and those unavoidable pitfalls guiltless men snag their feet upon.

It was not fitting to demonize authority's figurines. Having such little faith in the legality of devouring the governed prior to this encounter, I felt odd welcoming its attention. For the punishment system to do the dispassionate thing, when it was I who chose to do erroneous things so consistently, was not something I imagined they would entertain. Having said that, it did not stop me from making curled-up fists to slam upon the door in revolt. I demanded they be unflinchingly uncivilized in how they behaved toward me in a restrained and unnoticed act of defiance.

Hours passed before the guard returned to my cell, opened the door, then motioned for me to follow him down a long foreboding hallway. "I am taking you to appear in front of the judger. You will refrain from talking until you are asked to respond."

The hallway was godless and slender like the coiled embrace of a serpent's skin crushing the air from withering lungs. With each wretched step, I felt my insides becoming tighter and tighter as the enraged cauldron of regrets, shame, and haughtiness brewing in my belly over the last twenty-four hours began to erupt in mouthful size belches of puss and bile. I could not stretch out my arms nor could my hands take hold of the walls surrounding me without alarming the guard. It took every muscle in my body to trudge, to continue walking upright. The thought occurred to me that if I were to drop lusterless to the unkempt carpet below my feet, I would have assuredly fell into an aperture like nihility.

At the end of the hall was the courtroom entrance. The guard stopped and faced me. He motioned for me to enter the door leading into the courtroom. Sauntering into the courtroom regretfully, the chambers of legality were completely empty of breath except for me, the judger, the public prosecutor, and a court-appointed public defender. The public defender was a narrow man. His tiny eye holes were blank. His face was pale and mossy. His expression demonstrated what little regard he had for the justice about to be handed out. He smirked while reading the police report detailing all the reckless, thoughtless, and utterly reprehensible conduct I committed the prior evening, but it could have been from prior lifetimes ago for all I knew.

For the sake of my tumbling feeble ego, which receded momentarily into a tunnel of blackened self-delusion, my brain had abandoned all memories of everything leading up to the car crashing into the pole and a few slight hints, more like flashes, of events occurring after the wreck. Never underestimate the power of a full-on blackout drunk. The events transpiring along that dark stretch of road I traveled were much worse than I could ever have imagined.

I stood statuesque, gripped by a sense of billowing shame unlike anything previously known to me. "Death, dear death, I am knocking willfully at your door. Why, you fiendish beast? Why do you not answer?"

The judger looked at me with contempt and, with a mouth full of razor-sharpened teeth, began growling out the words, "Are you ready to stand and face your judgment, your punishment, your ever-growing list of self-accusations?" My mind was spinning. Thoughts upon thoughts were turning over in my head as to how I should respond before the words sprang from my mouth unannounced.

"Am I the accuser, the immoral, the insolent wetter who soils the linens of those asleep in beds of perfectly acceptable social discourse? Am I the villain perched atop the bell tower defecating over the heads of the gentle fellows trudging underneath and unbeknownst, those adorned in bright colored clothing dripping from the day's exhaustion? But please your honor, make no mention of the deeds I have tried so long to bury nor exhume the corpses I laid to rest in those graves shallow."

These heartfelt and misguided word's ramblings fell on my own deaf ears. Should I have foreseen the barbarous nature of my colloquy? It was mustered from a resounding and suffocating throat, that narrow passageway leading to a soul I no longer recognized, to potentially elicit legitimacy in the indifferent eye holes of judgment?

The judger leaned into his mahogany worn altar and slammed down his ancient hammer. The judger wanted to make me mindful of his virility. His overarching constitutional fortitude fell forlorn upon me like the world collapsing Atlas at last.

"You should be aware of the seriousness of your offenses," said the resplendent judger. "Lives could have been lost on account of your reckless behavior. Did you even consider the others who were trying to live productively? You are not the worst case I've seen before me today, but you are the most unaware of how truly worthless you are."

I chose to cautiously acknowledge the judger's acumen. When he spoke, a fear and trembling came over me. Without any prior consent on my part, the judger and public prosecutor began to converse with the court appointed public defender in a standardizing code like language used in their profession to abridge the normative hyperbole and to reflect disdain toward defendants. When the voice of judgment spoke, his tongue lashed out with hasty contempt, thick as an American history book.

The reckonings doled out by this tedious timeworn pedagogue reached back into the innocuous past, that way back callous age before men judged their fellow nomads. Submerged in a somber solitude, a miscreant with the slenderest self-reflective aptitude, I knew all too well my habituated imperfections and deficiencies. A roaming characterless creation tossed about bars while intoxicated men huff and puff without regard for one another. The lacking lingers in the mouth souring, waiting to defile situations requiring the conscientious handling of foredooming premonitions. Frigid and gripped by the grossly disfigured hands of authority. Charred hands of condescending regimes pour a metaphoric broth of dismembered frog guts and horsehair down exhausted throats while the evil twins, providence and imperviousness, sew lips shut to prevent obdurates from expelling the nauseating brew.

I balked in a not so polite manner, and before the judger could continue with the proceedings, I squealed in a resolute tone, "For God's sake, where the hell is that damn Rapture when you need it?" I truly believed I was the only proper transgressor amongst the courtroom attendees and would therefore be the only one not sucked up into Heaven's awaiting tranquility. This shortsighted exclamation of mine did not go over well with the judger. His face turned a bright red hue.

The absurdity of escaping my situation with the assistance of biblical prophecy was beyond reproach. I stood emotionless and tattered in buffoonery. "Shut your filthy God forsaken mouth or I will be buoyantly forced to gag you. Another word out of you could potentially seal the verdict," screeched the judger.

The judger was within his rights to use any means necessary to prevent any further courtroom outbursts. As citizens of this once grave nation, we unwittingly anointed the rulers of engagement. The legal establishment's superinten-dents use brutality to prevent one from speaking when unspoken. The privileged pelicans gag and restrain uncooper-ative defendants, those individuals who assert themselves with dramatic thoughtlessness. Disrupting the calm candor of the chiseled courtroom is frowned upon by pelicans. Those exercising upheavals toward constitutional guarantees dismantled become battered leashed creatures. Clamoring for causes to explain their insufficient existence, dogmen bark no more. Brutality and security, when faced with dissenters, become bedfellows sooner than later.

The meager voices of those trembling inside voting booths, casting empty ballots for policies and procedures gutted of all humanity, yet in their daily lives they cringe in recognition of their puss-filled deficiencies. The battered wear the fabric of individual dignity like a tattered flag swung over a dying soldier's last gasp. The coarse fibers of freedom inhabit all human depth, a profundity yearning for autonomy, yet finding itself expelled into a barren land of uncertainty. "Where the hell was that Rapture?"

The public prosecutor, with great reverence, reached into his briefcase, then unfurled the elongated list of criminal offenses for which I was being charged. He maneuvered courthouse friendly words filled with acrimony and legal bantering before returning to his seat. The flagrant legal establishment anticipates pleas of guilt beyond all reason from defendants unraveling. Neither myself nor the public defender assigned to my case had any idea how to proceed or who to reassign blame. The unkempt public defender dressed in mismatched clothing. His breath bore tinges of alcoholic residue.

Without intending, my reclining mind regressed from the unpalatable present, and drifted boldly into a cinematic inner journey over the tumultuous landscapes of green adolescence. My first distinct taste of disobedience. The middle school I attended offered a program, in conjunction with the local YMCA, to provide swimming lessons. My middle school was one of many in the surrounding area. Once a week for nine weeks, the local YMCA brought children from all over the county together to learn proper pool etiquette. They wanted to instill in us the wherewithal necessary to overcome the fear of drowning. Drowning as a means to escape adulthood is dreaded by those anemic in stature.

Instructors localize and analyze the swimmer's fear of breathing no more. The manuals place blame for its appearance squarely on the shoulders of repugnant childhood ordeals. Most of these unfortunates, these fear-driven children, were once victims of egregious bullies hurling them thoughtlessly into the deep end of pools. The lesson in how not to drown in deep ends at the hands of unfriendly oppressors was fascinatingly metaphoric and noteworthy for later in life ordeals. We were taught, unbeknownst to our efficient instructors, what it meant to be a modern man these days.

At one specific swimming lesson, me and two other boys from my school were the last three in the locker room. The rest of our class already showered and dressed and were waiting in the lobby. One of us, and I cannot remember if it was me or one of the other two, accidentally opened a locker belonging to a student from another school who was still in the pool. I distinctly remember seeing a large pair of bleached bright white underwear sitting so prominently in front of the boy's other clothing.

The necessity of underwear, specifically for the male, garners prestige for the gentile comfort it commands. The tight white cloth provides the scrotum with a layer of safekeeping from the coarse texture of one's jeans, the external climate and all unforeseen contact. The idea of destroying this boy's intimate garment, a tiny white object of coziness, something so sacred the boy's mother choose to write his name on the band to ward off wayward owls, symbolized at that very moment something shockingly erroneous in the world as seen through the eyes of an impoverished infantile mind. The laborious maintenance of a servant system. A chattel system of pernicious sanctuary veiled, concealed, and hidden away mercilessly from the prying glance of a passerby's curiosity. A serf system delivering gentle reprieves to entities participating in the glorification of self-worth dictates. Befuddled fools executing rolling rules. Fractured citizens scoff without ever questioning their own viability. Spiraling cultures demand allegiance from its members in the form of bright white undergarments worn.

At an unfledged age, I possessed a misguided competence for over-sensationalizing the profane. To entice subtle perceptions and florid thoughts with language symbolic and labored, then stuff the hollow beasts with extrapolated meanings plucked straight from cliffs and valleys where the mundane mind lingers. This unbecoming ability was not shared by many of my peers, nor was it something handed down from one dying generation to the next.

Without a moment of hesitation, I grabbed the boy's bright white underwear from the locker and walked copiously toward a row of toilets in the adjacent room. All three of us stood there not knowing for sure what to do or who should do it. My recognition of the event is somewhat muddled, but I do remember with certainty that we feared nothing standing around the toilet bowl.

No hypothetical consequences could deter us from this act of thoughtless absurdity, so I released those glistening white underwear with the boy's name on them into the toilet. The boy to my left pressed the handle and down they went, quickly disappearing into that nameless unknown. The awareness of being reincarnated from mere vegetation and thrust into a vengeful god-animal birthed from diverse unscripted yearnings at the site of the unremarkable nothingness came upon over me. Down goes that which wants to be no more.

We watched the toilet bowl fill with water and shrugged in assurance that someone's loins were going home unadorned. A perfectly absurd gesture from three exquisitely cynical youths unraveling. If the judger had access to my memories, I would surely have faced death by firing squad. Fortunately for me, memories are like unmarked graves others pass over without ever noticing the rotting corpses beneath the well-groomed ground.

The integrity of recollections regarding the receding days of childhood is tragically unreliable. Rote like rain rustling through storm drains to lower places. Impermeable to an adulterate consciousness. Unpardonable. To enliven pale passengers, bland reflections not deserving nirvana, is punishment for luridly hiding in the smog of declination. Mental memoirs pulse listlessly as they travel through decomposing brain veins. The once magnificent arrival of golden reflections aged, withered and became a mere hush against the pending winds of forgetfulness.

This must be maturity. It is not something to relish. What is a man without knowledge of history's horrors? Am I not an unquantifiable faction of the person I once pretended to be? A hologram of soot made to be dismantled with each gentle breeze. As I entered early adulthood, I fashioned myself into the form of a grotesque gesture balefully heaving itself toward the unfathomable sway of my culture. I was up for the challenge.

Like all brutal miscreants, I found no recourse in daily work humdrum and warrior weekends to mask the growing discontentment. I searched for something greater than myself, something that would ultimately destroy my puerile beliefs. Something to purge me of rightfulness and wrongfulness before consuming me. Idealistic men never return from self-induced odysseys to find themselves made whole as bread loaves. Their hurried return from battles victorious became the precursor for a lifetime of scorn. Even Christ was not welcomed in the town of his birth, and he was God as Man as sacrifice eternal.

The judger ordered the public defender and the prose-cutor to follow him to his chambers with a quick motion of his hand. I was told to remain seated until they returned. Their reason for huddling in the hidden room behind the judger's throne was not clarified. After fifteen minutes, they returned from the secluded room wearing large hats fashioned from old bones. The prosecutor and public defender proceeded to stand on either side of me while the judger returned to his throne, sat down, pointed at me with his thick ugly finger, then bellowed for me to stand. I stood up expeditiously as if pierced with a ferocious arrow in the rear.

The judger stared with eyes dreadfully splendid in their relief. "For your careless, thoughtless and malevolent actions toward your fellow man's completeness, I hereby sentence you to ninety days in the county jail where you will attend classes on conformity and banality and learn how to think for a change. Do you understand what I am telling you? Do you want me to completely remove your name from the book of life? Do you want to be given a chance to become a stranger at the beginning of a ravished sunset begging for the sands of time to swallow you whole?"

What could I have possibly said to remove all doubt from the judger's mind? I would not gallantly saunter along the narrow path of ascendancy. I would not become anyone's stranger, not even a stranger to myself, if I could help it. Digging deep into the pitiful bag of lies I carried within at all times, especially for occasions such as this, I pulled out an authentic hymn and began to sing. "Yes, your honor, I do I do I do hear you and want to lick your palms and oil your feet with regrets before bathing you in the machinations of a feeble existence. I will gladly join with your enjoinder in both mind and body. Your insignia will be my insignia. Being at one with your contract of repentance I pray. May I fall to bruised knees? May I give thanks and beg the magnanimous moon man to claw my unabsolved flesh with fresh claws covered in salve to heal infections forming? I give you my word your honorable honor."

I was led from the courtroom by the bailiff who was large and withdrawn. He took my arm, then used it to direct me down the hallway at a firm, steady pace. The bailiff stood outside the courtroom the entire time I was being judged. He waited for his turn to direct me.

I whispered condolences into the bailiff's tiny ear hole. I thanked him for leading me away from the mouth of judgment. The bailiff remained undefined. His reticence shattered my formless ego to splinters. He heard all the testimony, how I pontificated and postured myself with remarks meant for an unbecoming king. The bailiff was trained in the art of vindictiveness, but his absences of hostility toward me were specifically awe inspiring. His calm demeanor was itself a signal. A serene demarcation surrounded the horrid hole I was about to enter. Nothing left to remind me of home except the gross display of avoidance in the eyes of those dictating and demanding a servant like a charm be worn at all times to scare away the scarecrows.

A surrendering to the very essence of the situation was the only fitting eulogy I could muster. To trudge aimlessly through the ever-growing fissures forming between time and space, between man and animal, between last and first, between the tiny things that live within tiny things. I begged the everlasting hindsight of the universe to fashion a slight hole in its fabric for me to crawl through. A surreptitious amends to the gods of forgiveness, those genies in the sky who shatter the bones of a man's being, was appropriate. The leftover bones of the condemned littering skid row streets are gathered by unavoidable generations, then scattered across the unraveling floor of time.

As for the judicial process, I found it too vague in its application. Rabid dogs were more amendable to the plight of the underless class. I had no choice though. Only the dampened continually doubt the sanctity of divorce from sanity's revolving consolations.

Amen, I say to you. The bailiff took my wrists, slapped the handcuffs on, and led me out the front door, away from the courthouse and down encircling tunnels descending into the Cimmerian shade. Amen, I say to you.

It was noon when I first heard the bells chime from atop the town hall tower perched above the isolated gates of the jail. I was slumped over in my cell. When alone in one's cell and the door is locked behind you, an unparalleled conclusion comes over you, but it's not like the movie version, the sentimentalized cold steel gates or clanging bars or being assiduously swaddled by a most urgent loneliness; it's the realization that many men have resided in the very spot you now inhabit, and they too wondered if this was not an adequate penance. Freedom devouring citizens dream in isolation and live amongst ruins, but in confinement, there are no fake marble gods, no statues to honor with burnt offerings nor are there places, abandoned places, to lay one's head in utter resolve.

You gravitate toward the present to be present in all endeavors. Each breath exhaled becomes a nefarious opera performed for the trodden and discarded shadows once tucked away. The famished mind confounded seeks subtle forms of nourishment. The devouring restlessness dwelling in cement stratified tombs mortifies the disruptive temperament everlastingly.

Inside time unfathomable. A dripping eternity of slithering seconds spent reflecting upon cloven-footed things one could have done wishfully different. The ways one could have been emphatically different. We failed to acknowledge conspicuous people wallowing around our feet, and the floating fairies soiling our cotton sheets. We notice their pathetic prominence, all luminous and bursting, once gentle regards were replaced by a tumbling penumbra of discontentment. The book worn brain is a fitting cell for those whose thoughts wander along the parched stream bed of life, day after day, unable to interface with the surrounding world's horrors. Inside these four walls, there is time to relish the ridiculous and be unsaintly amused.

Every dull new day in jail is nothing more than a deeper dull regret for having allowed the prior dull day to pass without ever taking the time to let others know how little you candidly thought about their day-to-day welfare. One awakens inside to find nothing but his unseasoned will standing before another gaudy sunrise hollering indiscreetly, "I see you again barren host of purpose and careful calculations, and I do not care nor do I marvel." A developing sense of ignominy becomes one's life inside.

It is the sordidness of waking inside. We fling more "I don't care" transmissions out across the wobbling globe tainted by phonies wanting more things, to become combustible things without ever conceding to the light. Life behind bars festers like plague drenched rats. Inside minds are regrettable. Nauseating things abhorring the vacuum of nostalgia.

The most rightfully egregious things are formless and malleable. They suffer modifications to fit into the next keyhole, the next window ledge lock, the next lonely paycheck. The jail cell is not a metaphor. Only flowering academics reclining in leathery chairs, bending brandy to blistered lips, blistered from repetitiously pouring the noxiousness of life down their cauldron blackened mouths, would reference this sanctimonious literary tool.

The gray walls are not metaphors. The window's view, cluttered by bars, opens only to afford one the view of movable mounds of ants laboring aimlessly in the distant surroundings. They are not a metaphor. The guards scrutinizing inmates' rebellious whereabouts and ensure civilized society's rules are firmly entrenched and maintained, are not metaphors. The incarcerated exist in an overbearing expanse thick as a smug gesture.

The evening sun slopes under the dying sea, and nothing more is nothing more. Weary is the mind shuddering before the beatified mirror. Its fawning reflection is nothing more than an ensorcelled catalyst kneading years spent toiling to unearth an endurable foundation. We are taught to imbue sacred alone time with gifts of grandeur. Its redemptive quality falls on the heads of the newly poor and ferociously feeble alike.

Who ever truly notices the dying red hues of the leaves blanketing December's ground without knowing their pain? Who rotates in confusion? Who faces the outrageous past with its scorching vanity tugging on the contemporary?

I remained docile on my incarcerated metallic bed, drifting like dying light. Everything inside is unsympathetic and metallic. The incarcerated gather around gray metallic tables three times a day to swallow unrecognizable food prepared by inmates willing to exchange work for an early release. Thirty days of work equaled one day of early release. The tyrannical judicial system is never without a modicum of irony. More than a month spent inside. Time was spent counting the days impossible to replicate.

2.

When I was twenty-two, I abandoned the places I knew all too well. Crusted omen-infused localities of one's birth become mercurial under the skin after baking too long in the ovens of familiarity. My failing sanity necessitated a departure to some forlorn, funereal, and fusty place. To be shuttled somewhere far away from the stumbling staggering. The rote of living predictable damages the will to proliferate gorgeous non-redactable hues, somewhere an ardent willfulness and a salacious proclivity for the forgettable can thrive far from unapproving and prying public eyes.

To fund my passage to the new world, I worked for several months at a temporary county road construction job tossing leaves bagged and left on curbs by handsome homeowners into the back of a dump truck. It was a dirty, menial job. Most menial jobs are dirty.

I rode hungover in the passenger seat of the dump truck through streets of suburban malaise staring out steamy windows daydreaming about large fires. Envisaging tiny beads of anticipation pouring from foreheads of bloated faces for no apparent reason. The driver occasionally pulled up to a pile of garbage bags filled with rotting leaves left along the perturbing curb. Climbing down from my passenger perch, I hurled the bags over my head and into the truck bed. Sometimes the bags ripped open and spewed the grotesque odors of another autumn's yawn of decomposing leaves all over.

When the truck bed was full, we drove to the county's prescribed dumping site and deposited another regrettable load into a large hole dug for the compost process to occur. This meaningless work lasted from the end of October until the beginning of January. On most mornings, I labored with an older, overweight man who spent the first hour of each workday parked behind the local shopping center reading his paper and drinking coffee mixed with a hint of rum. The aberrant self-satisfying admiration for the life of a county road man was lost on me. The promenade of worthless wage earners rattling in time. Dining alone in old age homes.

We spent our mornings in the same ritualistic silence, avoiding each other's words and yawns. Sitting next to each other like dreadful mirrors. Any communication on even the most arduous or trivial level led to incessant chatting over the escalating burdens of home life and the family he managed so gloriously to overcome. A county road man with little interest in tomorrow's endeavors derailing his present serene morbidity. Enduring current calamities with an animal like tranquility obtained through years of back breaking manual labor.

A suffocating existence out there, waiting for autumn's end to arrive, yet still pausing reluctantly and periodically for another procession of empty hearses under another frosty sky. Was there more to my fellow passenger's existence than merely working himself to dust to ensure a deceit plot for his gravestone? "A man of fleeting time wears his hat low and avoids shaking hands with grave robbers," said the county road man.

Over the course of many autumn mornings sitting in parked dump trucks, attending rituals of coffee and rum and reading the newspaper aloud to himself, I warily accepted my fellow employee's moans and groans. He was not an example of modern man's ceaselessly swelling proclivity to darken their past. A eulogy in honor of his departure will be read slowly to a timid family of mice. They will remember his passive attitude and the way he never combed his hair after he showered.

No loud wailing will occur when they lower his casket into the ground. A low hiss will rise from the corners of the earth hole as he enters its seductive charm. His will be a death without dishonor. A bereavement granted to captains going down with the ship in speechless apprehension as they take their final breath.

The job suddenly ended one sloppy weekday in January. I injured my back tossing a rather heavy bag of soggy leaves. My back failed me in a human-like fashion and precluded me from further suburban labor with the glorious folks toiling at the county road construction department.

After a week or so of recuperation, my back started to return to normal. I caught a ride from my neighbor to the Greyhound bus station where I purchased a one-way ticket to the west. I could not fathom what would be different due to my noxious naivete, but I knew that it would be different, and that was enough. The buoyant air wallowing in from west coast sandy beaches was somehow cleaner and not filled with the soot of eastern repentance, or so I imagined.

Groping hordes of people with outstretched arms grabbing for the breeze lofting in from raging ocean swells. A land where the dastardliness of thieves, that inborn struggle to emancipate oneself from the burgeoning herd, was made dignified by the rhythmic nature of the marauder's code. A place where the demeanor of haunted fools is cherished and blameless like babies swaddled. Was it possible this plagued being becoming was at one time a perfectly good loaf of bread waiting for societal mold to arrive and fulfill its destiny?

Patiently, I waited for the bus to arrive on a bench outside the bus station. Staring down the road until, under the falling sun, I saw the approaching outline of my transport to the away place. It appeared like a resplendent chariot sent straight from the gods to puncture the stillness of normality consuming me.

Slow as time, the bus approached, and before long we boarded in a calm demonic trance. I dreaded the brackish possibility of sitting next to whining children accompanied by parents removed and vindictive, but as fate would have it, I sat sullen next to an elder woman with blue hair who endlessly complained about the insufferable quality of the seats and how her back ached when the bus maneuvered over potholes. For most of the ride, I gloated blankly out the window hoping to catch sight of an overturned car. I enjoyed accidents.

The ride was insufferable. After days of vehicular torment, we approached the horizon of our destination. I could not contain my enthusiasm upon entering the unfamiliarity of the background. To be no one, yet someone, some affliction of my own creation. Herald my own eugenically immune renaissance no longer mired by the whims of an anemic willed society. Discard the sheltered face of reluctance, a face worn down from time spent mourning over the imaginary facade of self-importance.

It all becomes so intimate and substantial in hindsight. The bus pulled into the gray station in the west, and the passengers slowly exited. Dawdling in my seat with impartiality until everyone had departed the bus. Savoring each moment before I figuratively abandoned the antiquated ruins of past lives upon entering the modernistic mind trap of contemporary men. Absurdity unraveling.

Envisaging newfound strifes and struggles between the falsification of self and the verification of grandiose ego mountain ranges, I was enlightened, then paused to make room for doubt. To discredit doubting Thomas while drawing water from his sunken soul valley was a purifying mental tool no true cryptic carpenter of men would leave home without ensuring this elusive hammer hangs from their work belt. You never leave lifeless yesterdays wholeheartedly behind. The torn ragged wardrobe of bygones unbecoming travels with you.

I stepped out of the bus and into the hot western air. The sunlight charred the final stages between my then and the present. The ground herded my feet tightly to ensure I would not be tempted by uncertainty and scuttle back onto the bus full of tomorrow's sorrows. Modernity had me. An all too relenting casualty born anew, beckoning under the westernized skyline.

For the first time in my life, I felt authentically homeless in a world full of welcome mats and flags flown at half mast, a professional exile unafraid of tomorrow, brimming with the gilts and glamour of a vagabond and the melancholic freedom of the underprivileged. A toddled wave of self-ambivalence washed away the voice I once spoke with as a child. I decided to grow a burrowing beard and let my teeth become yellow crust coated from prolonged hours smoking tobacco.

I stood motionless outside the bus station soaking in all the newness before wandering through the city full of stilts in suits and ties swung over necks passionately groaning as they ambled along in packs. Wafts of clean public air swept away my desire to breath. My reluctance to inhale exhale became eerier, weary, as if E. Poe hitched a ride on shoulders like a demeaning raven with whetted talons dug deep. The streets were estranged and effortless in their majesty. I walked timidly in a trance of delightful forgetfulness.

The buildings' erected preeminence lined the streets as far as the eye could see. I wallowed wobbly beneath their hollow glow. The sheer brilliance of their unique designs merging into one another was so foreign yet so inviting to me that the words of the prophets I could not muster. The stranger in a strange land metaphor entered my mind, but it could not contain the rapturous sensations swirling and contorted exhalations engulfing.

Mountains of buildings swayed above, covered in brown smog with moss gathering around their foundations. Endless windows glistened as they climbed toward the undaunted sky. They hung motionless like ancient doorways leading to remote clandestine worlds. Thrusting my nose forward to inhale deeply each new scent the city offered, scents ripe with foreboding fragrances to impress as well as to seduce coy minds.

Entering the first Irish pub I came upon, I ordered a double scotch and soda to celebrate my arrival. I drank audaciously and brooded over prodigal thoughts effortlessly. With an introspective glance in every direction, nothing drooping appeared vaguely familiar, nothing to remind me of being half stillborn, yet everything reminded me of being truly minuscule and woefully insignificant. "Another double scotch and soda please."

The doors of the pub opened and closed with a thunderous war song sound. The faces of fellow dabbling drinkers crowded together reminiscing over the day's divinity. I listened intently as they called each other by first names and swore outsiders were enemies flown in to contaminate the scenic malaise.

I belonged without knowing a single person. A discontent man is always at home amongst the fractured. I wanted to remain in that moment forevermore. To grab each pulsation of bare existence surrounding me and nail them down like fluttering erotic butterflies. To preserve in exquisite dead collection books, then open when things are not so agreeable in life. To be reminded that once I too was freshly laid morning dew.

The afternoon bowed slowly with each drink, and my soul was no longer weary. I stood from my stool and tumbled into streets glancing at half-closed windows enlightened with the theophany of an American urbane night. I needed a room to sleep off the scotch intensity before collapsing putrid like on the moaning curb.

I was not aware of my presences nor was I merely a numb character written by a frustrated novelist sulking over unfinished pages of prose. Will tomorrow arouse assurances when I awaken unamused? The first motel I came upon had a neon blue sign "Cheap Rooms" atop its deterring entrance. The message was fitting. I paid for one night, then fell asleep on a bed reeking of moth balls. Sleep that night was a tranquil respite seldom to be repeated.

With the most abhorrent emergence, the morning's stirring sky woke me in a furious hangover with the bitter taste of wretchedness on tongue. Impending sense of doom folded underneath head like a pillow formed from the hands of weeping virgins. I dressed, threw cold water on my face, then rushed out the room and onto deplorable streets screeching with cars, barking dogs, and pulsating pedestrians mesmerized on the throbbing globe spinning in my head, attacking all five senses like a pack of rabid rhinos.

To flaunt one's misspent juvenescence, all unfinished and moving in and out of consciousness, before the blissfully unaware waddling along city sidewalks with their eyes fluent in the art of being unobservant. This was the robe of essentiality I chose to adorn myself as I trudged slowly onward. To unearth a sodden insightfulness swelling within my chest like a colossal rock rolled over a mountain with measured cadence as crashing cymbals thrash the ground laying waste to all things frivolous and hermetic.

With a momentous and self-serving delusion, I believed all strange passerby eyes envied and revered my gait. I sauntered aimlessly along their humdrum lives. Envisioning myself a golden Buddha belly in their presence. Granting wishes and helping the sighted go blind. In need of nourishment, the hollowed out follow the hollowed out. I located a small out of the way deli and ordered an American breakfast of meat and eggs and toast. I devoured the meat. The bones of this city would soon show themselves to me and I wanted to be ready.

Days went by like all days do. Forlorn becomes as life breathes in and out the impenetrable air of mankind's miserable status amongst the crowded dying solar systems. Remaining bent on bequeathing to the world a slight nod of amusement, I trudged deeper into the obscure western landscape with its apparent mock civility and sacred putrid pundits of pontification drooling over the physicality of shame. I found a tiny apartment to rent by the week and employment moving furniture.

I found employment working for a company stripping dilapidated hotels of their interiors. They paid employees daily. We took out the carpet, the plumbing, the appliances, and everything else left behind by prior owners. On many occasions, we unearthed timeworn family trinkets forgotten left hidden within walls, along with bottles of pharmaceuticals outlawed and vexatious pornography.

Individuals with low hanging hands place gaudy preten-tiousness on things deemed inherently necessary and blissfully immoral, things obligating, and those nefarious things kept outside the public view. We fear hidden things, somewhat undisclosed things, will be seen disparagingly by all glowing orbs of neighborly judgment. It is better to conceal unscrupulous things in suffocating walls away from prying mores. What is even more revealing and incongruous than the effort it took to hide them carefully in seclusion is the way these same unmentionable artifacts end up forgotten inside the watchful wall's eternal silence.

The tragic owners of molding mementos deemed culturally underappreciated were compelled to make hurried retreats but not before abandoning delicate unmentionables in walls. The intimate family trinkets offer fascinating insights into the human psyche. When removed from both life and lore, important things become tasteless mounds of nothing. Inglorious gifts of taboo glazed perversity bore the hushed ignominy their owners kept hidden. Hibernating humans reminding themselves of their once scrupulous existence alongside bears.

The downtrodden survived the great financial depression of the early twentieth century hiding money in molding walls to avoid the inconsistencies of corrupt bankers. Aberrant behaviors seem justifiable and unhinged from afar. Isolated states of upheaval against the ravenous greed of faceless establishments takes place on every corner of every town, before another dawn washes them all away, again and again. These days, hiding one's solemn and intimate melancholy is hopelessly entwined with modernity's all-seeing computerized eye staring back into the abyss we have become.

On the surface, activities of concealing less than approved of presentations of self, advocating for a kind of willful dissatisfaction, though wordlessly communicated and proliferated, are not without merit or meaning. To shun others. To vilify those who posture. To banish the grossly unaware. The charades played by meager fools perusing affable functions, family gatherings or celebrations filled with unfamiliar faces, becomes lost in replication to a long series of ordinary clone overlords. What will become of this dematerializing generation?

We adorn ourselves in ludicrous shame for our unnatural desires and sexually awkward positions mixed with an escalating cultural escapism worn like the proper uniform of a soldier marching toward battles unwinnable. At the end of each workday, my fellow employees and I would divide the pills and porn and toss the family portraits into the trash heap of history. How truly American can one be?

General acquaintances were avoided. Intimate relationships with females frowning like empty vessels depleted and in need were not on my list of things. It was terribly difficult and problematic articulating my background story to others. Difficult explaining dead things to living things. The living things were too engrossed with the deceased to ponder endangered items of contemplation. Pompous thoughts subsisting off the pageantry of lore were not meant for hapless cogs surviving on the merriment of forgetfulness.

After work one Thursday evening, I sat at a local bar drinking heavily when a frightful woman in her mid-thirties sat next to me. She suddenly began a thoughtless conversation without my approval or even a hint of interest on my part. She continued to heap herself onto my presence dolefully like sour dough.

The devious female truly relished the thought of being headstrong in her presentation. She feebly tossed words around like swords puncturing the serenity of the bar. The bemoaning mouth she spoke from was particularly painful to look upon. She uttered in insignificant bursts of eagerness, sounding like a seasoned drunkard vomiting a bellyful of bemused canine urine. Her breath curled around my head as she spoke. It smelt like the waste of an old Labrador fed a mixture of aesthetic poverty and the humiliation known only to leashed creatures.

We spoke indifferently for several hours huddled around our drinks as the lights outside dimmed and the mood inside became beclouded. Our conversation was a one-sided loop of general nonsense followed by bitter conjectures, her lecturing me on the laudable glorification of being vagrant, and her theory of common sense being nothing more than purposeful stupidity. As the words fell from her mouth, they were often accompanied by saliva either dripping from the corner of her mouth or gleeking. This was unbeknownst to her. She impulsively tapped her long painted fingernails on the bar. It was annoying at first, but in time, her fingers began tapping out their own haunting vocabulary.

Listening to her ramble was like eavesdropping on a barking dog submerged under a pool of lukewarm salt water. A stew of sorrows gurgling with a hint of panic to survive bubbled toward the top of her face. I noticed her left cheek was drooping. The harbinger of duplicity resided under her movable face emerging into angelic brilliance one second only to alter into rabid wolf fangs drawn.

I quickly became infuriated and indignant on account of her mongrel breath. Scoffing at seriousness, I settled back into the bar stool envisioning throngs of wayward lizards walking across the desert floor aimlessly. I occasionally contributed a word or two, but she did all the non-stop gore-filled talking, incomprehensibly and without discretion.

After four or five drinks, she leaned toward me as if to tell me the world was going to end and, with the least amount of words her feeble mouth could utter, said, "I usually don't have sexual relations with strange men I meet in bars, men who are mistakes or who have hidden agendas." Was this an interrogation or an invitation?

We drunkardly gazed into each other's eyes waiting for the other to break the uncomfortable silence. I could hardly contain my contentment for her quivering lips. I warily declared, "I am not as outlandishly forsaken as I appear, though I am rather dull down there."

The little I know regarding the ways of women should never get in the way. But what is to be done when an earthly figurine, ripe with lascivious hues, captivates one's waltzing across the timid life unbridled, bent over, slumped, and shivering for recognition? A woman of low moral standards with much alcohol in her belly invites me into her apartment after the sun has fallen. Wise not to refuse this libidinous souvenir nimbly. I considered the obscure nature of my fluctuating pulse as I began weighing my options. Who would vacate a room ornamented with an unclothed form without enduring the triumphant macabre of baring oneself? To be in the presence of pornographic brutality and to embody one's own misdirected animosity toward the history of physical perversities. The inhumane way of probing for consolation in the arms of another while thrusting your gentiles into their gentiles, until you both forget you're even vaguely human.

When one achieves the fruition of this disastrous and lewd genital craving, and the need for this ugly unification is left foaming and frothing on bed sheets steaming, the last bullet of a thought your reserving achieves its' total consummation through ego death. Do not mistake this for a suicidal serenade for the sexually repressed and moldy. This outdated practice of fingerless foreplay is not of my design. It is more obtuse. A life of infancy unaware of its passing strikes at the most ginger of susceptibilities. Given the hopelessness I was feeling, I relished her invitation and stood on my own hind legs. We luxuriated in a carnal divertimento, performed in the nude for the benefit of those suffering in mute agony, then demarcated each other with a soft sigh and a nod of reassurance. It was unforgettable.

With full knowledge of our fiendish physicality spilt, and its demented remains reeking of bleach, our forms became forms quivering and reddish in glorious places like radishes ripened. A dripping wet liaison. We directed each other's hands suffering as they passed over the firm pulsing flesh of the other. The terrible other who, upon removing their withered "no trespassing" sign, allows you to walk with muddled boots over their undulating face parched, all withdrawn and scorched, as you penetrate the simmering room within. And to think, I never took the time to ask for her name, but she had not bothered to ask for mine.

A mating dual where monumental pleasure driven deep into the opponent's belly ends in a whimper walking away. Knowing death might soon greet us tomorrow, we spill our soulless selves onto caustic carpets, forsaken and inexcusably hostile. I took one look over my shoulder as I left her apartment to make sure she was still breathing. Unfortunately, she was staring at me as if to say hurry away devil before I beg you to stay.

"Hurry away before I vandalize your simplistic grin, before I dig dull talons in and pluck out eyes so you won't see the empty spot overtaking my recoiling bed. An unholy relic of my loneliness displayed," said her convolving eyes. But I could not wander anymore over her silly femininity, as if to do so would invite ghosts, grievous and forlorn, to have another bite at my tongue and leave me once more dreading the doleful day of my birth. As I walked down the street in a half-hypnotized state, I happened to glance ahead and to the left and noticed a small dog playing with a red wheelbarrow.

Days slither as days do, like moseying sounds purring out of an old trumpet horn left to rot along some remote highway leading to another burnt village full of yesterdays. A sound to rouse remorse. There was an agreeable comfort in knowing it was the ultra-violent days, those hypnotic note-like days. A cluttering and clanging of ritualistic notes for the Pied Piper's song played for an obscured generation in the age of rats. Each trudging note played from the Piper's haunting pipe follows another trudging note into desolation, into empty space and profane time. We fall prey to their whimsical slandering. The sound becomes soundless. The soul becomes soulless. To demystify our present and purge our forgotten. Days proceeded like this for me. I petitioned the endless winds for some inaccessible refuge to wither away in declination. An eerier glimpse of prevailing denials pining for more to adhere to confronted me with bleak familiarity. I trembled patiently for the next note to arrive, to be roused, and to be unsaintly incensed.

While working one tediously hot midday unloading unused upholstery from an apartment complex on the west edge of town, a fellow employee asked me for a cigarette. He told me his name was Mark. He worked at the company for several months and hated it. I gave him my last cigarette. We stood sheepishly outside along the street as he smoked. Mark was a tall, thin man with an especially atrocious intimidating smile. A slight hint of trepidation resided on his brow. Mark appeared ready to lunge with a hatchet if questioned. Castigated for lacking earnestness or handling discontentment with the television-infused world benignly, Mark seemed stern in preparation for a deliciously savage response.

After talking about nothing and meandering around nothing, it suddenly occurred to me we both lacked a certain concern for daily hygiene. I confided in Mark that I would go weeks without brushing my teeth. I enjoyed the jagged textured film left on my teeth after spending days smoking non-filtered cigarettes and drinking large quantities of brown beer.

Though I clothed myself in eternal sensibilities, I frequently embellished myself with armor-encrusted teeth glistening in the grotesque to prevent wayward female tongues from slogging the sanctity of mouth's interior. On more than one occasion, hackneyed women stumbling and stammering in another dingy down and out bar commented on how woefully my breath offended their gentle repose. One drunken brooding beast of a woman announced to the surrounding crowd how my babbling enunciations flung about in her general direction was like being sufficiently sprayed with a fine mist of rancid repulsive sewage. The banality of talking over drinks quickly ceased. Receding into the slow bar loneliness I masked with each gulp of intoxicants, loose libidinous conversations with unwelcomed female mouths dwindled into the faint nevermore.

Mark was in his early twenties. He lived with a girl named Cindy and her six-year-old boy named Pat. They lived in a small project apartment nearby overrun with dealers, users, usurpers, and tattered prostitutes doing their doings. These festive individuals also made up the majority of the tenants. Mark informed me that Cindy's stepfather owned the apartment building and they stayed there for free. After work, Mark invited me to his place. We purchased a twelve pack of boozy beverages and a pack of cigarettes for the evening conversations unraveling.

The apartment building was exhausted. It was painted a dark defecation brown color. Some demonic force decorated the brick heap in three-day old diarrhea. A foul odor lingered in the air. Mark knew all the substance dealers peddling out front. We stopped to talk with a few.

I quickly realized Mark and I both relished ingesting substances of all varieties. The more ego damagingly delirious the better. Mark made a quick purchase, then we proceed through the apartment gates toward his second-floor door. Cindy greeted us. She was also in her early twenties, thin and donned a natural looking long flowing blond wig.

Apparently, when Cindy was much younger, she had a serious bout of bone cancer, and after several rounds of chemotherapy, her fallen hair never properly grew back. When I asked her about it, she told me, with a shivering grin, that it did not bother her tremendously. She always wanted to be a blonde. Pat was sleeping when I got there but was awakened by all the talking. He was a fragile looking boy, as if he had spent years sour from sickness. He spoke softly and ate rather quickly.

After we grouped around the table drinking aimlessly for a bit, Mark and I went outside and sat on the stairs. He told me he met Cindy in a strip bar several years prior. She was working behind the bar. Mark ordered several drinks from her before building up the intoxicated courage to introduce himself.

Mark would then frequent the strip bar as often as he could, but being low in finances, he could only afford a few drinks and never permitted himself a dance from one of the gleaming girls. After a month of almost daily attendance, Mark asked Cindy out for dinner. She accepted.

Cindy was living in an apartment her stepfather procured. Cindy and her stepfather once had a sexual encounter and, because of which, he now paid for her room and board out of a fastidious sense of guilt for matrimonial deceptions. She was only sixteen at the time. The dread of pedophiliac cravings being exposed coupled with an angry wife uncovering his lack of marital discretion were enough motivating factors that the stepfather willingly provided Cindy an apartment far, far away from the family home. I cannot blame him. Cindy was genuinely alluring in a post-chemo kind of way.

We sat for a while discussing the nature of the world and how little we thought about our fellow man. It took four beers each before Mark dug the little baggie of treats from his pocket. We immediately indulged until we were heavily substance confused. It goes without saying, unhinged individuals in the grasp of hell's unhallowed clench, those quizzical folks presiding in mentally diffused states, form common alliances to deal with the daily hindrances of life.

Some minds are just better aligned when strung out, leathery, and gnarled beyond their normal thresholds. The chemically-induced mental reprieve allows for unfeigned conversations to entice more depth and longings. A swollen psyche sickened indulges in talk of ego banishment without cowering in corners. A frowning verbal fortitude is required for gazing cross-eyed into blackened cracked mirrors of misapprehension.

We talked about historical inaccuracies and culturally approved emotionless states of despair pushed upon timid heads huddled. Mark was into being abysmally authentic even though nightly folk would rather not entertain this notion. But with any great windfall, inhabitants of this brittle gobbling world will scuttle out of the formless past and float upon hedonistic waves until sandy beaches of forgetfulness covet those poor thrashed bodies time so unceremoniously belches. Mark quizzically canvassed the rolling sky as if he were about to pray or in anticipation of an unseen comet plummeting toward our heads. He turned toward me and said, "it's nice to have someone to talk too, someone who is not afraid to expose the reprehensible underbelly of disappointments and not cringe when they find it a communal experience. I would very much like it if you stayed with us. We have more than enough room and you would not have to pay rent, just help out with the utilities and food and we can reside evenly together, all four of us."

The first thought which came to my mind was whether Mark was hitting on me, and then, if Cindy would dispute this decision. I waited for him to say something else. He was benumbed as if struck over the head.

"Sure. But what about Cindy?"

Mark told me Cindy genially mentioned to him, when I used the bathroom earlier, that she found me innocuous in appearance and wanted to know more about my clock ticking. She thought I was sorely sympathetic with a calm lackadaisical demeanor. Mark, in a matter-of-fact manner, then quickly pointed out that he and Cindy were not bound over to each other and were open to all sympathetic experiences.

The uncommon arrangement was a lot to take in, and being so flushed from mind-altering intoxicants, I quickly agreed again before apathetic thinking mechanisms identified cracks in the veneer of kindness being presented by Mark and Cindy. What else could I do? Looking back, I understand Mark was much more misplaced than I and needed a formidable fellow traveler to gain some sense of placement amongst the fractured souls haunting his awakened dreams.

A willingly debauched falconer to complicate Mark's falcon was being asked of me by the great hindsights in the sky. As much as I was overcome with appreciation for the amiable gesture, I was torn between being with others and wolfish yearnings to be alone. Also, in the short time I spoke with Cindy, the abhorrent fervor to eventual see her naked body writhing underneath me already began forming in the back of my lascivious brain box. A warm female body, an unhealthy child, and a friend of misappropriated intentions were all being trundled into the vacillating sphere of my growing uneasiness toward the animal kingdom.

The notion of family formations dangled before my calculating mind like kindling before the flames of eventuality. The appropriateness of belonging. The cadaverous familiarity. Jarring monologues concerning preoccupations with gregariousness was not foreign to me; it was a trembling perfidious vocabulary I seldom uttered.

Mark was an accurate person. He was incapable of pretending to exist for the sake of another. Nor would Mark risk losing any ground fearlessly seized in the battle waging within, a mêlée fought for sanity gained while trampling unreliable emotions. Mark was not a common type of person striving for gluttony, for the attainment of worldly mementos, for greedy things full of apocryphal fangs and fading privileges. He sought a sorrowful status attained after long hours kneeling before toilets regurgitating proper theologies, swine-like consumerist ethics, and mores remote and unattainable. Mark gave the impression of having a certain foreknowledge regarding my disgust for rambling through life without reinventing oneself in the image of blood sucking bats or ravenous ravens. He was correct.

Conformity to an unrelenting system of authority was unbearable, a society of forged falsified words carved up like Thanksgiving birds of prey. We were still for a bit, both transfixed in the privacy of our own intoxicated head spaces. As we stared off into the distant demoralizing view beyond the apartment complex stairs, I delved a little deeper into Mark's offer, but was firm in my resolve to dissolve there amongst them.

Could I stay with Mark and Cindy and Pat without becoming another familiar hoax? I questioned my hurried response. Mark and I were both so remotely adrift on debilitating waves of mind-altering substances to respond to anything demanding our full attention. Life made it all the more puzzling.

We opened the last two beers and drank them without uttering a word. Just as we finished our last beers, Cindy came out and nestled behind us. She had a maternal look about her, a complicated look of restlessness. It was as if Cindy already knew my decision. She wore contentment in an unfamiliar way. I felt the ugly urge to caress her face, to hold her hand or put my arms around her and make a wish. She leaned into the space between Mark and I and said, "Is everything okay?"

Nothing okay was the shivering hole I burrowed when saintly alone and covered in the vague and unnecessary. The well of twisting sorrows from which I bathed drained me, but the way Cindy's amenable lips parted as she spoke, her tiny blue cotton shirt, so delightfully tight in the cool evening air, removed and dispersed all desire to be dislocated from her presence. Cindy's perfectly pointy nipples pressed toward me as if ushering the way to enchanted forests of merriment closed off. I laughed the vile laugh of a mad villain committing to memory his plan of world domination before saying, "Yes, I mean yes to you both." Mark looked at Cindy and nodded his head. They were pleased. Residing together we agreed as the little boy deeply dreamt inside on the couch unaware of my continued presence.

"Would you like me to get you gentlemen some more beverages?" Cindy asked in a tonality so kind to my ears.

I handed Cindy a twenty-dollar bill and told her to grab us a twelve pack of beer and to get herself a flower. She coughed as she stood. Cindy walked across the street through dilapidated men dealing little packages of pleasantries. Insidious substances designed to remove all doubt from wandering minds. Many more vile pipe dreams throttled as the professional women laboring along streets in slim fitting spandex shorts and low-cut shirts, wave at hissing cars traveling lonely roads to nowhere.

Mark began to speak stoically in a completely unexpected vernacular. He spoke like a poet gargling a mystic potion of bat wings, dragon's breath and the scorched pages of a passion play written before the gods of idolatry reluctantly walked the earth. Mark spoke in a premeditated manner.

"Cindy is very special to me and yet I do not love her in the least. I know it is inappropriate in our culture for a man to discuss intimate matters between himself and the women of his affections, but I want you to know my intentions with her and her son are not at all perverse nor do they stem from a self-destructive nature. They are like hollowed-out sentiments worn about the neck, necessary figments of certainty for a depleting grasp on sanity. An abhorrent point of reference to cling to. Concealed landmarks meant to disorient the wary traveler.

"Cindy is like a picture whose frame is molding, like a cherished memento clenched when quivering. When I plummet to my lowest, she ordains my trembling and faithless fingers with her vague way of reassuring me. Cindy assures me of the ephemeral quality of thinking disorders feasting upon the fictitious, the fabricated and the damned. Cindy can, with an effortless grace, penetrate my inner most and ever-increasing insoluble insecurities.

"Cindy's kind dejection is very calculated, very useful and similar in essence to a decomposing map found along the road to pathetic places traveled alone. She fortuitously furnishes me directions forward into the meanderings of a callous and indifferent world. I am constantly made aware of how Cindy fluently describes herself in relation to me, how she riddles her body with riddles, tormented passages of words leading nowhere, and at times epitomizes my misguided softheart-edness. I trust you can, with a commiserating reverence, embrace the nuances of our living arrangement."

As Mark spoke, his arms floundered about like oars maneuvering on a drunken boat of blurs. "I want to be sure you understand what I am getting at so if the moment arrives, if Cindy were to, for a lack of a better word, 'embrace' your embraceables, and you found yourself wanting to 'embrace' her embraceables, do not hesitate on account of my behalf," he said.

"You see, I have little if any concern for Cindy's physical appetite, her morbid sexual sustenance. The way I see it, you are here, a form amongst our ever-evolving forms, barren and monstrous. You appear to be a man of multifaceted sureties. If you find yourself sensual disfigured by the "otherness" of Cindy's presence, the alluring warmth of her prying physique, I only ask that you be genuine with your longings. I will not stand in judgment, nor label you a trespasser promenading carelessly over fertile fields, one who trudges inanely through exotic meadows of borrowed bodily delights.

"Cindy's architecture houses a salacious sophistication known to all fallen deities. She is not some vacated temple of antiquity to be pillaged for its golden eggs. Cindy is not unlike the formidable altars for kneeling in anticipation of receiving all-healing consecrated hosts. Does this make sense out of the ridiculously unfeasible? Am I making any sense?"

It did, but it didn't necessarily engage me enough to fully appreciate all the finely tombed nuances Mark was endeavoring to convey. He struggled thinking long term thoughts. Mark unquestionably demonstrated the hopeless wonders of phosphorous philosophic contemplation. Mark valued his roaming intellect like fading artists clutching chisels when standing before unblemished blocks of marble.

An unexpected occurrence amends. Mark altered the manner in which I differentiated laboring individuals based solely upon their declining occupations. This was not the same person whom, hours before, dressed in sorely tattered jeans, a loose-fitting shirt with the words "Eat Butt" emblazed on the back, and a hidden predilection for unkempt human hygiene.

Was this the same sulking employee I labored alongside, ripping and tearing down apartment interiors?

Like a primordial bolt of lightning tossed from the obsolescent lands Zeus ruled over, or being endlessly trampled under Apollo's polished chariot, the infantile egg dwelling within, unbeknownst to me, splintered wide and the yoke from a thousand thriving obscurities, those torturing bedfellows fumbling under midnight covers with fingers perverse, split out and evaporated in a divine like burst of clarification. It was sobering. A somber sign. This arresting apparition slithered from the tar sands of time to devour me thoroughly as Mark turned his face and spit on the ground.

In a hesitant hum, I hastily explained to Mark how I so desperately trammeled myself with separateness. All far-flung inaccessible judgments toward egregious things were dropped dead on silver streets. Since leaving the old bones and entering the new geography of both landscapes flourishing and soul creatures dividing, I trudged further with brickless feet. I told Mark how difficult it was illuminating my inclinations for Cindy, a woman known for only a couple of hours. Finally, I hinted to him the euphoric effects of intoxicants consumed were wearing off and necessitated a refill.

It was unsettling. Attempting to befriend another man in general was made even more vexing upon hearing his complete contentment with girlfriend engaging in acts considered bodily betrayals of the most salacious sort. It was all too unreal to grapple. The unexpected, the bemoaning sense of not belonging and obscene flesh mandates were all heaved upon me.

Even though thoughts were tangled motes of thorn laden vines, yawns of vagueness within began fleeing. Conspicuously held doubts dissipated like diseased vermin scattered over corpses plagued. Cindy returned from the store and walked up the stairs toward us with beverages in hand. Her lush lips parted in a smile, eyes dancing and the softest breasts floating before me like seraphs before the great finale. Did Cindy even notice the facial modifications I painfully ventured with each softly tossed expression of longing?

I encountered Cindy for the first time like a newborn being reborn. She was not wearing a bra. Cindy's lickable nipples were both benevolently protruding. I wanted so desperately to caress them between precarious lips, but the tottering toddler inside only wanted to suckle.

The vividness of the next several weeks spent with Mark, Cindy and Pat is something I recall with inordinate fondness. We became very familiar. We ate together, worked together and slept together in the same king size bed during humid summer nights without air conditioning. Pat slept on the couch like a dreaming tiger.

Our daily conversations revolved around the possible, subjects relating to things possible, and minor hindrances with regards to space and time. The delirious drinking and illicit substances indulging were constants throughout most of our evenings, but they never became the focal point of our existence together. A movable bond is formed between roaming outsiders when the mirage of sanity collapses and is replaced by the poise of one being misplaced, being diseased and alone and crippled inside without remotely believing the luminosity at the end of the tunnel was anything other than an approaching train.

Cindy donned an unrelenting dignity. It dispensed from her lifeless frowns like celibate streams when she spoke of times in life when she sought more for herself, more for her child, and how the solitary emptiness goads her to pursue relief in the arms of another, even if the other was just another repugnance yet discovered. She confided intimate details to me when Mark was not around and held my hand as she sobbed. Cindy's far away eyes stared off into corners of empty rooms pleading with imaginary liberators to come and transport her away from ghoulish beasts consuming her breath. The goats of men besieged her trembling mind. I too glared disdainfully into those same corners but beheld nothing other than arcane paint peeling from tainted walls.

At times, Cindy became so intent on obtaining a response from the unseen, all-consuming presence she believed was mocking her. Her swollen eyes restlessly searched the emptiness unraveling. Cindy's woes would dissolve and dribble down her face. They mixed with tongueless years, haunting reservations, and rushing streams of noxious tears igniting the whole room in bursts of unbecoming pageantry. An inferno born from redemption not requited. I spent my time with Cindy so remorselessly, so genuine in my wanting to be inside her flesh covers. To endure the temperateness of her body before me and to appreciate the agonizing attempts made to rid herself of the past, I followed the path of least mental resistance.

The psychological mementos of yesteryears carried Cindy away in bouts of thunder and tranquility while I remained unmoved beside her. Could I be that abhorrent element for her, a thick clog to cram into that proverbial tunnel between the here and the then, to block its entrance until she burst open like a dam left long ago by a generation of deceased beaver kings befuddled? Together, I envisaged we would find a new hatred for overt righteousness. The sheer intensity of our sexual exploits alone would surely rip us to shreds. Her son could gather the shreds and use them to fertilize the flowers weeping in the yard.

But what about Mark? What about the swindler's guilt boring its smug dagger into my side as lustful apparitions enveloping me? I could not be his friend and foe simultaneously. Prurient prospects of sharing Cindy's pleasantries was something Mark first mentioned. He could not to be bothered with her titillating niceties.

The taxidermical manner in which Mark stuffed his dead feelings to make them look authentic and lifelike was foreign to me. I reluctantly heeded the cacophony of echoes blaring in my head. I surrendered to the inaudible, the temperament, the acceptance of pettiness, the vague traces of consciousness, and those tiny gestures hung from refrigerator doors to remind and discourage all fleeting attempts to alter the almighty Tao.

The shuddering birth of today gives way to cycles of life and cycles of death. The resurgence of the trudging forth cycle, fate's fastidious finger pointing toward the grounds outside spectral towns, allows for time to intensify its wounds. The undernourished, scrawny and rawboned leaders of sheep demand the walker of worlds bury the last of the boring childish memories before history's forgotten revel in them. Lay claim to inherited death rituals overdue. Fabricate a new insane world full of lies from the still-simmering clay of the old world mote. The old mote ran dry. We must fashion a new legion of falsifiers to replenish it.

Ludicrous. Everything is maddening and ludicrous. I lay waste to the past confounded and embrace the present unbearableness as though my today tense were a sincere slab of dough flattened under a malicious baker's rolling pin. My despicable depth of self became a dark fed mushrooming inaccuracy becoming. Endlessly unsure of everything except my incorporeal being trembling and faithless. I worked with Mark during the day and fell prey to delusions of Cindy at night.

The ever-evolving fluctuations between a man finding solace in a sanctuary of non-attachment and a woman clenching at her foreboding chest heaving. Self-condemnation is the brutal trough from which the insecurities of mankind's oldest foes and heroes alike dine. The child was the waiting world watching the three of us wandering toward the ubiquitous cliff nestled along an unnamed rye field. Pat was the tiny catcher with tiny arms and we were the three unhallowed appetites frolicking madly in a field of hardy annual grass.

As another day of work ended, Mark and I stopped at a Chinese restaurant, sat at the bar and ordered drinks and appetizers. We each had around a hundred dollars but decide to skip out on the check. We began talking generally and laughed occasionally. Mark looked out the window contently before saying, "I want to leave, to go somewhere unaware of me, to start again. But I do not want to take Cindy and Pat. Do you think I am selfish for not being concerned about what happens to them?"

I hesitated before answering. "I know how it was when I too had the overwhelming urge to leave the familiar redundancy, to just get away. Not that I'm saying yours is similar to my situation, but I do know the cruel disposition of one wanting to be novel, even if it's merely a geographical change one seeks." I think it best not to provide nor provoke justifications for another man's actions even when asked for, haphazardly or wholeheartedly.

Trepidation is a well-grounded response. It's not wise to give credence too carelessly to a man in the trawls of a decision especially when it involves complementary consequences. I could not pretend to understand the full ramifications of Mark leaving behind Cindy, nor could I truly appreciate the reasons for contemplating an unaccompanied life.

My answer left a remote look in his eyes, as if he hoped for more acceptance, some sense of approval, on my part. "You are not content with life as it is, Mark, and I do not intend to sound dismissive, but what brought me here, the need to deconstruct myself, then reassemble myself far from unapproving eyes, does not provide me adequate knowledge from which to advise." He seemed to appreciate the sincerity of my reluctance to counsel.

"Cindy has been alone before. She comes from much worse situations. She thinks more of her life with you now than the continued burdens of our faltering afflictions. We are going nowhere and she is, just as I am, an undomesticated servant searching for a more potent fix," Mark said with a contorted look.

What did Mark just say? Did he intentionally slip in something regarding Cindy's wanting to be with me? I felt my chest cave.

My throat became insanely dry, like gravel was being poured down it. A flicker of possibility lodged in my throat. What did Cindy say to him?

"Mark, I don't understand what I have to do with you and Cindy entering or exiting each other. I feel slightly contrite. Being venerated by Cindy's allure is one thing, but I'm not sure what we're talking about. I'm not serious about my unraveling presence. I lack all utter sensibilities necessary at this odd moment to even begin to bleed. Maybe I should leave before I become an excuse for either of you."

The numb weight of my tongue twisted the nouns and verbs and phrases. Servile sentences fell from my baffled mouth, nonsense ramblings over twaddled ramblings eliciting a vile string of nonsensical syncopated sentences. My hands waved recklessly. My skin became taut and beehive brittle. I was under attack. A swarm of moralistic bees stung, scoured and surveyed. The discomfort was trampling.

With a serene look of compassion one would not expect, Mark reached across the table and held onto my hands, cleared his throat, and said, "It's okay. It is completely alright. You have done nothing but provide me and Cindy with months of amazing, authentic companionship for which I'm so grateful. You arrived without any preconceived notions. You knew what you were getting involved in the day we asked you to stay with us. You shared yourself, your dreadfully repressed recollections of agony, with us. You opened up about the unsettling murky landscapes you've traversed and did so without the least bit of doubt we too ventured into our own shadowy places."

When did I do these things? With what acumen on my part was Mark referencing? When in the company of the trodden, the overtly ruined, it is easy to believe we are all cut from the same distant diamond. Even if the glistening stone is worn around the necks of those in the murkiest of swamps, there is little hope of ever finding a way home. I must have displayed my gaping neck wounded. They must have smelled the caustic blood coursing.

The waitress asked if we would like the check. We nodded in the affirmative. When she disappeared into the kitchen, Mark and I got up and slowly sauntered out the door. Once hitting the open air, we sped away, moaning like drug addled wolves on the hunt, until rounding a row of apartment buildings far from sight. It was nothing like words. It was hopelessly alive.

When we returned to the apartment, Cindy was waiting patiently with a hint of foreboding draped around her neck like a deadened, drenched albatross recently plucked from a stormy sky. Mark smiled at her apathetically and in a soft voice announced his departure. "I'll be back tomorrow to get a few of my things," he said to Cindy, who appeared paralyzed. Mark grabbed his coat and old baseball hat and walked out the door, to where I did not feel it was my place to ask.

Unbeknownst to me, Cindy and Mark previously discussed his moving on and leaving me to guard over the tomb he so recently constructed. Cindy started chain smoking cigarettes. The room became permeated with swirling smoke rings. Thick rings upon outer rings of smoke maneuvered themselves into all four corners of the room. A hint of forbidden delirium in Cindy's eyes saturated the rest of her face as if the movie she spent hours watching in nervous anticipation reached its resolution. The hideous denouement arrives with its many twists and turns. The end of laughter was approaching in its cathartic finality. Cindy wanted to be ready.

I did nothing. I waited motionlessly for Cindy to orchestrate the symphony of befuddlement surrounding us. A benumbed boy and breasts beyond belief became the moment. Like musicians tuning instruments in joyful expectation of the conductor's lionized arrival, I knew the music we were about to perform would be operatic in its brilliance. A magnum opus. Classical in its composition. It would stand the test of time. Surpass the likes of Mozart or Schumann in the annals of classical tympanic pleasures. The mind of a fallen man strung out and in danger of being seen overlooks the insensate ends, makes just that which is not at all unjust. Those tormented sensations of self are merely reflections of one's visceral titillations being served their due.

A lifetime of laborious trivialities and mitigated hindrances overcome are quickly ameliorated with the sexually sanctified look a woman gives before bedding begins. Her eyes instruct and inform you. She is going to be a defining experience, one ruling out all other possibilities. You have no choice but to drop your head in veneration as she kneels before you. You stop questioning the lonely whys. She takes your hands. The aphasic tranquility afforded to the deceased comes for you through ethereal lights leading into the next world free from all ruinous mourning.

With a calm demeanor, a woman banishes all the remoteness experienced in excruciating silence. You gingerly encounter states of temporal contentment mentioned in the ancient texts. You understand the Eastern state of inwardness. Commune with life's fleeting emergence. Hail with great gusto what was always meant to be before the exalted and irreverent flood.

Rise above any and all disquieting occasions with an uncluttered voice and wings perched headlong into the abyss of pure artistry, pure proficiency. Could any point of reference embody and epitomize the anticipatory seconds before being undressed and facing each other's naked textures? Standing before the original sin, the origins of all sinful, fleshy behaviors, the history of licentiousness stands with you. The manner in which Cindy arose from her chair with arms temperate and shrouded in suggestiveness left me solid in low places.

Cindy waltzed toward the bedroom. I followed her, transfixed and unable to speak. Then it happened. I became a thunder god in male form, golden fortunes lay at my feet, flourishing kingdoms of the world begged for forgiveness, the moon winked, and the sky became my breath.

We laid next to each other without the need for words. I spent an eternity dreaming, studying the tiny space formed between Cindy's lips as she smiled jovially. I wanted to tell her I was completely over myself and all the pitfalls of my life. I wanted to let her into my murky basement to cleanse it in some sappy amorous way. I closed my tired eyes and blissfully drifted off, hoping never to return. I quietly yearned to die heroically next to Cindy's motionless curves, then leave the withering world on guileless notes played for a deaf tribe of dancing ghosts.

In the morning, a pounding on the door suddenly awakened us. Cindy got up in a hurry and raced to the door. Before tumbling out of bed, I heard the most lonesome soul-eviscerating shrill to ever rattle the gates to Elysium, a blessed location for the comfortably dead. The forgetting of a vengeful universe known to me the prior evening was hideously disem-boweled.

A horror had happened. Woefully wandering into the living room area, the first thing scorching my sight was Cindy's face torn apart and shattered in dreadfulness, two frowning cops standing at the door, and lingering blissful bursts of elation departing for evermore. The police informed us that Mark hung himself in a motel room down the road.

My memories began to devitalize and brutally rupture. I turned inward and became a fabricated form unequipped to ingest the demise of Mark's untethering. Somberly surveying the four corners of the room, ridiculing specters split from behind my eyes and paraded about to taunt and torment the appalling hush draped over all wishful things.

Dire speech swelled in my throat like a prickly pear. All movement became slackened and abated in rolling waves of anguish. Cindy was not crying. Her eyes turned to blood. When she looked at me with those abandoned blood-filled eyes, I was consumed by a desolate sense of guilt unlike any before, like being dipped into a cauldron of boiling oil, then nailed to a wall and left to dry. Crispy was my crackling character.

The police required someone to identify the body. They asked Cindy to come to the station with them. I told her I would stay with Pat while she was gone.

I could barely identify my own decompressing flesh at that point in time and thought it best if I remained behind to look after the boy. Cindy nodded timidly in acceptance, then put her coat on and followed the police officers to their car. As they drove off, a tremendous urge to vomit awakened in my belly. An overwhelming urge to just decompose and allow the vicious vultures of judgment circling above to hastily devour the rotting lump of flesh.

How could this have happened? Nothing in Mark's presentation of self could have led anyone to believe he possessed any inclination toward self-immolation, to go somewhere beyond the pale mask of morning, to be something impervious. Mark ended his flimsy mortality and began that lonesome pilgrimage beyond the eternally remote.

During our drunken stupors, Mark never once mentioned any fondness for hanging in a dingy motel room down the road. But, if he did, I was always so ferociously consumed with aberrant thoughts of sexual debauchery with Cindy to have even noticed. Constant ruminations castigating. Sorrowful tunes turning over in head reminding me of the mounting dreadfulness curling itself around sluggish loins slung low. Ineffectual. That damned hour when shouldering the mounting inefficiencies my distraught character craved became comically disengaged. A clown without a crowd to amuse.

For this, I am henceforth a fabricated fragmented man. The molding flesh I wear will evermore be draped like a ragged garment reeking of the unspeakable spoken. A man can never truly be godless, to be beyond all reconciliation, until he dismembers the embryonic, the emergent fetus within him. The metaphoric hands of insincerity carving up his own aborted self. An act so vile and so irreproachable. Enter again the proverbial mouth of Mephistopheles. Become the sauntering nausea bringing forth lifetimes of vomitousness, slathered onto the unsuspecting world of mindless men and red ants alike. A fabricated fragmented man.

Pat was still asleep. I did not have the courage to wake him. I never fully understood the relationship between Mark and Pat. Was it a father/son relationship or merely mom's next lover type of friendship? Neither mattered now. I decided to wait until his mother got home to let her explain the travesty.

I sat somber like a boring monk. All empty and timeless, I tried as earnestly as possible to come up with some explanation, some free-floating justification, to understand Mark's self-inflicted descent into bereavement beyond the recourse of dying embers. There must be some way to frame his actions, a way to relieve myself of burdensome feelings associated with the finality of a friendship.

I could not distract myself from trembling long enough to consider how the Cindy separation might have affected Mark's overall contentedness. Maybe the reason for his death was not so complex. Maybe he ate enough lymphatic slop at the troth of worldly discontent, a pig's meal made from the king's sickly discarded scraps, that his souring stomach became so desperately bloated with oscillating anxieties and worldly regrets it finally burst wide before the unknowable. With a coward's foresight, Mark doused himself in self-wrath to be released.

We would like to believe those taking their own lives do so to remove some primordial pain from existence's silvery screen, but it is more barbaric than a tiresome movie trailer can contain. An error of vanity constrains the noose worn around immature necks, then pushes them off the chair. The unfortunates living diligently lunge into the inferno's abyss, a place of honest reckoning. Drawn toward the scathing flames of endlessness like mad children, the lost brood forever writhe to pacify ceaseless urges to be away from another atheistic day with humanity.

How long must mankind stand before unavoidable chasms and utter prayer upon prayer for silly redemption? Who will open frowning eyes as morning approaches? Searching fruitlessly for the clown's path, twined minds march toward a wrenching absolution. Procure the holiest of deaths. Is not this formless life worth so little in the end?

Do we not enter this frigid world still-born of meaning, dwindling in open-ended explanations and engulfed in tongueless trivialities? Do we not end with the same resolute privilege? To be one of Plato's forms and not the creature in which they were implanted, or not to be? How lacking in forethought is the assumption that to follow one's intrinsic judgment is comparable to being a pirate flag of an idea meant to ward off the banality of men with tiny feet?

Bedaub the timid minds of mice men with this notion, each step taken is not one given, but one stolen. The penalty for this clumsiness of thought is not unification, but conclusion, finality and the rogue misgivings of the embittered. Wanton and beguiled creatures purging themselves of fire, making room for the more insidious gestures. Enough of these thoughts swirling around my hideous mind, they did not, and still do not, grant me a hint of the foretold serenity accompanying an aging man as he lays down in the dust of history. The woman I so recently shared an exquisite slice of heaven with would soon be looking into the dead face of her befuddled suicidal lover. Remaining fossilized on the couch musing, I was a lonely walrus crying rain tears. A daydream within a daydream without any inclination to ever awaken.

And so it was for several hours. Time can be unusually sensible when licking your wounds, tasting the bitter and the blatant blood, knowing your recompense comes in the form of proverbial hammers to nail down yesterday's hell hounds barking. I suddenly and without any unrelated realizations began to grasp that which was not meant for me to grasp. I felt my heart turn a pale blue, thickened, then became a glazed over doughnut with sorrow filled sludge at the center. The thicket covered ground petitioned for my return.

Shuddered and shaken as the entrails of my life pooled in a black bile, nothing came to cleanse, nothing came to bathe calloused feet in the oil of forgetfulness. Must we resentfully trudge the unbridled sequence of appalling pauses until death delivers? Acting wholeheartedly without hesitation, we champion another metaphoric existence along another bloated parade route down another fading highway to nowhere. The doleful day of devoutness with its betwixting opus ended a long time ago. We are merely the fleeting echo, the faint bark of a decomposing dog buried many millennia ago in a gross graveyard no one visits.

When Cindy returned home, I was still sorting through boiling memories. Her disapproving guise curled my insides like Cain's toes when God asked him where his brother was hiding. What whimsical proclamation could possibly make sense out of the super surreal stage Cindy and I floundered upon in utter dismay? What words could be spoken to forever remove the look of sheer defeat from her drowning face?

The inability to deny the unadulterated abominations residing under Cindy's eyelids was all-consuming and all-damning. She walked toward me, then sashayed right through me like a tree's shadow before the lightening splits it in half. Cindy never blinked. She continued to the bedroom and fell upon the bed. Cindy was saturated with tears when I finally entered the room. I heard a slight mumbling in her voice as she repeated Mark's name over and over until it was like a drop of boiling tar being steadily dripped onto pale forehead. My thoughts twisted and swaggered like dying pelicans falling from the searing sea-sky onto sweltering seashores. The room became thick and pungent with ghoulish emotions unraveling.

The entirety of this horrific spectacle is eternally seared into brain's unholy place. One of the worst ordeals recalled when desolate under a howling red moon. I stood by the side of the bed without saying a word to Cindy. At some point, I turned quietly and walked out the bedroom, picked up my coat and a small bag of dirty clothes waiting to be laundered, then continued out the front door.

As I walked down the steps leading to the entrance of the apartment complex, I knew I was not going to turn around. I knew it was over. Rolling bliss was an ephemeral and barren thing. Like sinister, scouring winds rumbling over deserts of lifelessness, this whore of a sensation was subject to the hideous ways and means of disorder and folly. The morning sun was bitter and blistering upon broke down shoulders as I walked further from Mark's finely constructed tomb. The surrounding oven air cooked the unpleasant day.

God, as I remembered, no longer desired my presence. The Grand Inquisitor in the sky told me to crawl down crumbled streets in a constant state of disbelief and never wake, never shake off the cold coursing life, never glisten again in beds of golden women made from bones old as fossilized stones under the bridge that links this miserable world to the next. I was the punishment for being myself, a frame of reference people would point to and say, "that is the thing that caused all the awful things." And I would agree, if only I cared enough to agree, but instead, I would leave once more and find a new home in the next town, in another state, in another abhorrent world full of repulsive fangs and obnoxious snakes clothed in eternal sensibilities.

I did not return. Never went back to find out how Cindy and Pat were doing. Never considered how they were somberly subsisting without the flowing crimson robe of a vengeful creator to cling too. It never occurred to me what Cindy might require to sort out the ending of life incident. A slumped shoulder to rest her exquisitely depleted head upon. Cindy deserved someone to make right the deeply ingrained wrongs life bestowed. Leaving was reprehensible, but I was amiss.

The world went void of any remarkable exultation. My continued presence in Cindy's life would have only reminded her of what she had, or could have had, before the plunge, before goatmen with amber horns and teeth fashioned out of barbed wire introduced her to sadness and sorrows, before tomorrow's burning branches entangled what remained of her faint ardor. Unbecoming was not something to relish. A listless *cul de sac* for Cindy to stack up her dirty little secrets as time turns the awful into reusable lustrous ooze was not for me.

Oddly enough, though immersed thoroughly and without any suspension of disbelief, I fathomed the complex nature of guilt and shame and gluttony, but I surreptitiously yearned for nothing other than another ethereal escapade with Cindy's firm breasts and the congenial sense of sacrifice her lower regions imbued. It haunts to this day when alone and shallow in my gravely life. A distressing state of blackened frostiness, a darkened hue so horrifically brilliant, a sickening singularity forged from the bitter hands of forefather, F. Bacon, found me shrouded in pernicious flames. Convoluted deliberations ransacked and rumbled my skull. Cerebral sirens lulled with thoughts odious and abandoned. Fledgling things morphed into ailing frogs fumbling in pools of Mark's hanging gore while I peered through a distant forgotten window watching as Cindy's stepfather stole her virginity over and over until the fog of waking was no longer welcomed.

I could never return, as desperately as I desired, to those passing inglorious places of yesteryear's fumblings while figuratively bending over its wide gaping grave. The echoing voices of spite announced my misplaced obedience to the awaiting world. I found the nearest highway and started to thumb for a ride. It was early afternoon when I received my first ride.

A woman in her mid-to-late thirties pulled her rumbling auto over and gave me a ride. She bore the striking appearance of a women whose drifting life was exceedingly atrocious. Beaten repetitively about the face by life's demented backhand, superstitiously and figuratively, to mask any signs of prolonged exposure to enjoyment. Beaten down by the fitful fists of fate. She traveled with her ten-year-old daughter hovering in the backseat singing twangy country songs for empty hearts. There was a half empty bottle of cheap vodka in the center console. She offered me a drink.

I downed a big gulp and passed it to her. I could tell she already consumed large portions of vodka because her lips fluttered like dying butterfly wings. She spoke of how lonely she was, and the long years without allowing a man entrance into jagged nether regions. She lowered her voice to a faint whisper and said, "On no uncertain terms, I have not stopped thinking about the possibility of pulling the car over at the nearest rest stop, find the nearest bench and unload years of sexual dysphoria."

Would she leave her daughter alone in the car while lustful humps devour rest stop benches? Placing her tiny forehead on window. Witnessing the falling distance as I entered mother from the remote rear. A quizzical line in the sand which I may, or may not, attempt to cross. A movable line's accurate location, though, was not always apparent after many inebriating drinks. When her hand sloppily flopped into my lap and began fumbling for the concealed, a swirling shameful sandstorm suddenly satiated the car's interior. A line crossed. I told her to pull over. I got out, thanked her for the ride, then watched as they traveled further down country road songs.

The next car to pull over was a young couple in their mid-twenties. They were headed north to visit old college friends. Their rolling laughter filled me with ease as the car trudged onward.

The man asked if I smoked, and the girl handed me some fine green earth. We inhaled, giggled, and conversed about nonsense, the dying world, the plight of under-educated masses and westernized demigods laughing at the cynical bastards we've become since their departure. How little they noticed the horns growing from my forehead or the way my tongue was starting to fork. The skin of a serpent is never quite as apparent to the one it's about to strike.

They did not know of Mark hanging in an empty old motel room alone. They did not know it was I who stuck swords of eternal damnation into Cindy's unblemished marrow. Were they waiting for me to tell them, to release guilt upon them and barely come clean before changing the whole backstory into some pompous fable full of dramatic proportions and wild propositions to entertain as well as to wheedle these little vanity-schooled bees? The miserable hysteria of today becomes the miserable of tomorrow without the hysteria, but in its place, we could leave tiny pieces of bone from mildewed braincases along forgotten paths to distract ourselves from being finer selves. Stale breadcrumbs left by a dying breed of wingless bird men.

Maybe we could all shave our heads and free the lice. Maybe we could chisel out those memories which punish and chastise. Maybe these two careless individuals cared less about trivial glimpses of secular gladdened lives.

There must be indulged inhabitants reveling in life carelessly, and confidence filled dwellers wallowing in the plight of the indulged. There appears to be a lot of regrettable individuals finding life merely a long-prolonged preparation for the hell to follow. This sordid lot saturates days trifling with sorrows, unfolding unused napkins, and glorifying sadness-sized statues of self-hatred. They devour the lugubriousness. They mainline macabre things, diseased states of consciousness into awaiting varicose veins to numb themselves before the gaping mouth of Gehenna. Its dreadful arrogance has no dominion over them. No novice disillusionment unfurled at their feet. Nothing loathsome applies to these calm colorless creatures. The notion of unremitting perdition disturbing to the very core excites these anemic beasts. The shocking awe of forever torment is nothing unfamiliar. Another dried out, utterly boring twat tumbling along. The great and apparent dichotomy grows like moss over tombstones.

We drove for hours talking aimlessly about the current unease my two traveling companions were experiencing. Anxious and unseasoned, they were heading back to the college town they once called home. They spoke of many wondrous memories made so innocently sweet by the light of youth.

For no apparent reason, the female loudly confessed her virginity lost to an engaging man she met at a college after hours party. She was introduced to him by a fellow English major. They both enjoyed reading tireless poetry. They met at a college coffeehouse called the "Raven's Den" to indulge in institutionally bent conversations revolving around forbidden poetic aspirations, how little people concern themselves with little words, and the plight of working bees. After hours discussing the ins and outs of Westernized Literature classes, the glowing gentleman asked if she would like to go back to his place to read his sloppy poems. The female then softly whispered toward the backseat, "we went to his apartment, indulged in a bottle of red wine, were caught up in the venerated rapture that is John Coltrane, then drifted into the godless glorification of jazz skedaddling."

She shared all the delicious details of their lustrous evening entwined. After two glasses of wine, "My Favorite Things," and sardonic surrealistic verses, the man leaned in and kissed her softly on the shoulder. She mumbled something about the burden of virginity before suggesting entrance into amusement parks hidden.

The total and absolute blamelessness of a young lady's naivete is wondrous, not delusional, not something to maintain in a well-mannered repose, but something begging to be ripened by the disturbing glare of carnal delights. "So, he put his hand on my chest and began to stroke my leg with his other hand," she said. Stricken by her comical callousness, I leaned closer to hear the salacious story unfolding.

The suggestive narrative apparently pushed at the driver's buttons. She was trying to get a rise from her male friend. She was baiting him to intervene. She taunted him to open up about something other than his utter lack of concern. Meanwhile, I blithely bathed in her bodily niceties lingering around the car's interior like alluring perfume drawn from Aphrodite's seashell. She did not have to awaken anything murky inside me.

The green earth smoking intoxication, and the way she spoke in tiny hiccup like breaths, replaced the torrid of trembling memories of Cindy, Mark, Pat, and little girls singing county songs while drunken mothers drive forgetfully down insanity's highway. She expertly enunciated the juicy parts of her story, the parts where she allowed herself to be ravished by Coltrane's horn, clothes flung around the room, and her clean linen insides penetrated by the big red wolf for the first time. She would never feel the dislocation of youth again.

The baleful male driver then sententiously interjected, "I am sure we do not need to hear the rest. It is obvious, and trifling, how you relished yourself. Nothing you could say would be anything different from anyone else's first experience."

He was wrong. I wanted to pummel his doughy forgetful face. Need I remind him that some of us did not mature nor gleefully grow in cultured gardens surrounded by succulent ladies disseminating delicious delights? Some of us were the prey of vultures. We, the hapless and volcanic ones, were not fodder for a willing virgin's rapaciousness, but worn-down worm meal. Disencumbered from the world of pallidness. She became silent. An unmistakable urge to violently thump the driver about the head so as to cause the car to wreck came over me. To see his tedious face to go through the front windshield boiled in my belly, but it was not to be.

We pulled into the small college town. A cauldron of unfulfilled depth. The rain-soaked unraveling roads were smoldering and slick and shining under harrowing street-lights. The driver pulled the car alongside a house where his friends lived. The female sat quietly unamused.

Neither of them even asked me if I wanted to come with them. Why did they not drop me off along the road? Maybe they knew something I didn't. Maybe the female wanted to hear a story about deranged damsels stripping away the freshness from my form. An amorphic man molded from a lump of clay at the hands of egregious virgins.

I exited the car stumbling and followed them into the house like a long-gone friend returning from the murky storm of juvenescence. I should have said something, but the dreadful anticipation was too much for me. It might be a dungeon home housing a group of serial slaughters to overcome me, voluntarily drug me, drag me into a cold basement torture chamber, then hack off arms and legs. Stacking the fresh carnage in the middle of the room, they would dance around dismembered body parts and naked torso in pure exaltation before devouring the flesh.

I would not have minded. Detached from lukewarm banality and tepid states of squalor, to be the ravaged dinner for unsavory educated tribesmen dancing might be enchanting. Upon entering the house, I was first greeted by succulent sounds of trumpets blaring, somber and funereal, with hints of tormented tenderness. The melody was utterly desolate though accessible. Shrewdly placed notes to reassure listeners, those astute in multicolored hyperbole, the fruitless gods of antiquity were currently cadaverous bedfellows. We were then joyfully greeted by a few of their friends. Everyone was vigorously animated and overly friendly to a fault.

As the night progressed, I lost track of the couple who brought me. They were mysteriously absent. One of the men residing in the house introduced himself. His name was Andre. The members of the house were looking for another roommate, and he wanted to know if I was looking for a place. And just like that, I found a spot to sleep that night. Andre introduced me to the other roommates. They were all in their twenties and were all fond of consuming large amounts of alcohol. I would, for a brief time, fit right in.

Sometimes things in life just happen. Someone says something in jest, and you say something in jest, then the something becomes life in jest. All ridiculous necessities, poignant agendas and issues requiring long drawn-out conversations, considerations and decisions made, were just not relevant. A willing acceptance of the fleeting moment was tantamount. Nothing determines the fragile of mind. Those yearning with blank faces and a resolve to not delve deeply into the masquerading abyss of human determination will find a home amongst the broken. It is preferable to not decide, remain ethically paralyzed, allow the rush of novel experiences to eclipse the maddening decision making processes, and be defiled by pure uninterrupted adventure.

The night awkwardly proceeded with the consumption of heavy amounts of noxious beverages mixed with hopeless dialogues reminding me of Mark, who I imagined was fighting off huge armies of sea people in the dark ocean of death. There was continuous talk and talk and talk amongst my new collegiate comrades over the unfiltered machinations of minds unraveling in murkiness. The verbal trudging through wicked thoughts such as these required a tongue fashioned out of bronze. We required bellies full of booze and acrimony to make sense of distilled discrepancies between the movable now and the frozen then. So overjoyed being in the presence of people harboring hidden pretexts, I swiftly removed several layers of skin. These were sore bastards soaked in bleach demanding acknowledgment for simply being alive. They performed like grotesque monkeys. Lambasting and berating each other with nostalgic words and fleeting images garnered from worlds they were forced to inhabit. Wilting worlds made from clay and wax.

As conversations regressed, the household inhabitants ushered themselves back into less than sympathetic corners. The drunkard's long crawl back into pendulant rooms, unnerving and bleak of purpose. At the perfect age to become grossly aware of the nothingness, that singularity of thought festering in minds harrowingly inept, my liver, and its growing reluctance to imbibe, grudgingly gave its blessings. I was undeveloped academically but could carry on with those practicing verbal sorcery. It does not require much to punch trifling holes into slippery arguments heralding certainty, authenticity and clarity of thought. I trudged fastidiously. Headlong into the futile abyss, I cultivated the diseased predilection needed to drink oneself into obscurity.

The after-midnight hours spent shivering horrifically awaiting the cantankerous kiss of the sunup succubus. Falling into a dreary slumber. Engulfed in dreams of wayward college girls tremendously far away from the safety and surety of their patriarchal homes.

In the morning, I tumbled off the couch in the main room of the house. The detestable taste of strife and fatigue coats the hungover tongue. I was not yet a formidable friend of death's fumbling fingers. Silence silhouetted before the mushrooming sandstorms swirling within.

The two individuals who brought me to the house were gone. I never bothered to pay homage to them for the ride and the story of an awkward faced girl losing her virginity to Coltrane's horn. In a strange yet self-indulgent manner, I applauded them when I appeared alongside the road they were traveling. They found me. Driving toward the next town, picking up another street walking Camus, indulging him with a ride to nowhere in particular, then, a second before they turn onto another all too familiar endless highway, they would give pause to remember they left me behind.

Andre burst down the stairs screaming about forgetting to go to his probation officer. Apparently, several months ago, Andre was drinking with a friend, and when they ran out of alcohol, they broke into a Catholic church and searched in vain for the holy blood of Christ. In a drunken state, they tore the place to pieces like two frenzied Dionysian madmen until someone heard the noise and called the authorities. The police were enraged because of the sanctimonious way Andre explained his unlawful actions as being that of a disturbed sinner trying to ascertain the divine in man. But, like all reluctant sinners, Andre fell short and did so without deliberation, without belief in mankind's riddle-filled misguided ventures, without doubt in the mighty one. In full pagan glory, one not granting pardons and forgiveness, we all fall short.

The police, in their ego-blank perfection, did not appreciate Andre's inebriated sermon nor the context of God in man in delusion and swelling self-denials rolled up into large golden goblets of wine-drenched religions. Andre and his friend were subsequently arrested and taken to the station to sober up before appearing in front of one who sits in judgment, who passes sentences with the mighty hammer of laws, those coy worldly punishments which, in Andre's case, include a year of probation along with restitution.

The driving nervousness and shooting panic Andre demonstrated as he ran around the house knocking on doors, looking for a ride to his probation officer, was absolutely invigorating. Being under the pernicious probation system of a sinister court is tricky business. Enshrined jurisprudence, with its righteousness guard dogs and vile motes filled with the soul eviscerating phlegm seeping from the incurably enslaved, ensures punishment's dripping dagger sooner or later stabs, punctures and pricks that which does not obey. This never mattered, nor did the rule of law matter, to a mind as unavoidable as the one the dungeon demons bequeathed to me. Why should the higher powers in flowing black robes tower over our supposed collective insanity?

We, the festering citizens of the wayward and beguiled nations, are always at an indefensible stalemate with existence. To find punishment an inevitable state of being is not unusual to many who live without recourse. Always aware of being judged and judging those seeking to cause ruination until you forget something, something about social politeness, some concern for others, but the other's maniacal suspicions are too great and time is too short. Hatred is a lamentable place to raise long-legged children. They will grow into formidable shadows. The corrective light blinds eyes birthed from dark passageways. The constricting arms of false liberty draped over fragile shoulders tightens around nibble necks until they abdicate.

Andre was so impatient to meet with his eventual condemner. For allowing me sanctuary, it was my duty to assist. Dr. Jekyll called and Mr. Hyde answered. When ugly Satan, the king of all that ever goes wrong in life, shows up on your doorstep as a gorgeous twenty-one-year-old blonde with huge begging breasts and a fragrant ass immortalized in the stars, you should never doubt the sincerity of being unholy. As for Andre, that blonde showed up in the form of my utter lack of concern for civil obedience.

"Let's steal a car and I'll drive you there," I said. Having never considered the trudging consequences of rabid-life choices, I was all too ready to disobey the law, to vilify authority's embalmed grip and burden a world deemed graphi-cally simple. The thought of criminality easily passed over Andre's decision-making mind and into his pragmatic mind.

"Do you want to know something about how to make your life livable?" I said.

"No, no never," he replied. I agreed.

We began walking down the street like absurd pirates without ship. We looked for a gas station to find an unattended car. During the walk, I posed a question to Andre. I wanted to ask him before but was not sober enough to remain in a lie. "Have you ever considered your life as something which, for the betterment of the rest, should be locked away in a Parisian café, to be in a constant state of righteous literary incarceration?" Andre looked at me for a second, then continued walking. It was an honest question.

There was no carefully crafted plan on how we were going to temporarily borrow a car. The idea came forlorn and quick without much in the way of thinking deliberately. I told Andre it needed to be abrupt. Pick a color, then pick a make, then find it. Nothing happens as planned and this was no exception.

We approached a gas station. There was a small black car parked next to a pump. The owner of the car went inside to pay for gas and left his car running with keys in the ignition. How perfect. In a second, we opened the doors, entered the interior, put the car in drive and away we went. Blood boiled. Tides of guiltless perfection attained. Every lurid sensation titillated.

The thrill criminals get from breaking the law is an old and verifiable condition. The fastidiousness of life is painstaking. Pay close attention to its passing. At any moment, time might easily expire without your awareness. The day to day duration of bland barrenness eradicates all authenticity. Pledging adherence to oppressive laws while obeying authority in all its grotesque splendor is worthless beyond fabrications allure. It weakens the vindictive loins and breaks down the indigestible personage.

We drove dauntlessly. Immune to the crippling fears most find abhorrent when doing wrong things for wrong reasons. After fifteen minutes, we arrived at Andre's probation office and pulled into the parking area. We were surrounded by parked police cars. Flaunting overtly obvious things in plain sight without a single person questioning their nefarious nature is attained with little effort. One must know before one sees.

We got out of the dissolving car and left it dead for the pitiful law officers to find. I waited in the hall while Andre visited his probation officer. He was gone for under ten minutes and we were off again, but this time we walked aimlessly away from the probation office gloating at the very capriciousness of our criminality.

We decided to stop and abide the somber calling for demented drinks. The bar we entered was an old, rugged-man type bar. They sold three different kinds of beer. The hum of music from an era lost in the mundane consciousness of time asphyxiated all the impeding discreetness the weary patrons could muster. Never could I recall feeling so ironically alive and so without even a hint of concern for having just temporarily borrowed someone's car without their approval.

Andre and I laughed and talked over the absorbing ordeal. The exaltation of thievery was raw and palatable. We nurtured and relived each moment with comically clarity. Sanctified the memories of brazenness for having interrupted the machinations of law. Disruptions for the inevitable unraveling.

Thinking back on that brittle day, a rabid friendship forged in delightful debauchery, glaring and brilliant in its deprivation for anti-authoritarian conduct, nothing could touch its scenic malaise. There was a time when benign honesty between unfortunate people was distinct and well defined. We promised to nevermore be so villainous again, but secretly wished we could have driven mad all night under a deaf sky rolling away. A pilfered vehicular absurdity traveling across forgotten country highways to find pale hitchhikers willing to travel into mad wantonness.

After four beers, we left the bar and entered the surroundings as tangible men drunk on spirits of disillusionment and near-death experiences. We talked of starting a poetry magazine. We envisioned writing hidden messages in poems to conjure the melancholy of our age. We talked of pale-mouthed girls whom we wanted to devour before time fashioned their tenderness taut. We wanted to live in a blindfolded world unable to see incoming traffic.

A devious pursuit for pure divine madness driven from sheltered lives. Laughing lunacy angelically fondles folks slumbering, shelters their lionhearted fondness from day-to-day-old civilities unbecoming. A shattering derangement gives birth to aborted explanations flopping from rustic rusty wombs. To exist on a winding thoughtless path carved from the eager hands of the regrettably self-undiscovered was not a path to be trudged. I never decided to become anything remotely interesting. When the thought occurred, of building a bigger, better bomb for all, the blinding madness of an eternally recurring future was artfully enrapturing. Instead of dreading its gray tone slowness, like a shadow living within you, the unfriendly without within, embrace all the witching seriousness before the licking tongue of uneasy slumber beckons your final breath.

Andre and I stumbled sardonically as we waltzed. Our speech became slurred and blurred and stopped sounding like verbs and nouns, but inebriated baritone sounds, palpitating, shameless lyrical fangs shredding the awkward nature of our disappointments. This was not a moderate sound with much humor, but buoyantly disembodied sonic hues infected from the viral loaded rats we devoured. We enjoyed each other's mistrust for the Holy Western thought process which consistently and thoroughly provides citizens a reassuring cycle of boredom until death.

Not a single thought of Mark underground nor Cindy violently moaning all day or night. Another gentle reprieve. I wanted to tell Andre all about the many unexpected and frenzied experiences I shared with them, but I also wanted their hallowed ghosts to go, to leave the humid cemetery constructed to house their memories and expedite a gratifying entrance into a lush forest of alcoholic forgetfulness. Time spent drinking away time. Musing on immutable tomorrows and tomorrows where blistering is no affliction to be overcome, but a cure from the weariness weighing down stranded sufferers. I told Andre nothing about Mark hanging nor Cindy shivering with child. He never asked about my disintegrating bookends.

We walked for an hour without ever noticing we arrived at a street near our house. We were glib charlatans. As we turned down the road heading home, I said something like, "Could you imagine what the heavens would be like if they allowed us to design the buildings?"

"It would be a place of vanity tenfold and full of wine and songs about reconstruction and burdened beings without feet to walk on," he remarked. Andre was not meant for mankind's lustrousness nor its mocking rectitude. Two merry poets walking toward the unraveling void in masks horrific and, at the same time, existing in rapture laced translucence.

That night I slept like a vindictive shepherd who sent his flock to the butcher to be slaughtered and was free of their presence. The morning's cruelty arrived all too quickly. Everyone living in the house were full-time students and were gone to morning classes when I stumbled downstairs. My room was on the second floor of a three-story house. There were three rooms on my floor and a bathroom which was never used. The entire house was so filthy most people who visited would refrain from entering.

One of the roommates would clean his mountain bike in the tub and leave the mud in the tub until it became a tiny indoor garden bed. The toilet did not flush and was full of vomit from the many party guests who could not make it down the stairs and out the front door. The shower on the first floor worked but was just as disgustingly vile. The hair cleaned off the drain was piled into the corner of the shower until there was at least a foot high of hair, mildew, and a small roaming band of tiny insects. Overall, the house could best be described as having a demented character, one offending weakness yet instilling courage in the hearts of those devotedly frail enough to enter. This was not something I found unpleasant. Instead, I viewed the house as a hideous defense against all that should be. The cleanliness of life blotted out from the world in bugs, mildew, and vomit-filled toilets.

There was a rickety old couch and a mattress on the floor of the room I occupied. The mattress stunk. It was left in the rain for forty days before the prior occupant dragged it back into the room. The mattress was discolored from urine stains. It smelt. A tormented bed for torturing medium sized animals in a ceremonial fashion. I covered it with dish washing powder, then layered it with six or seven fitted sheets I found in a basement closet. After several days, I did not even notice the smell nor did I care what I was sleeping on, just that I was sleeping on something other than the ground outside or underneath the rotting carcass of some down and out vagrant.

I sauntered around the unremarkable town, and the rolling green college campus, to gain a better understanding of what little I was lacking mentally. The town was not very small at first. It seemed like it went on for miles and miles aimlessly until I lived there for several months. The college was filled with peers, victims of my generation, who seemed bent on academic destruction. They possessed the unflinching willingness to figuratively end their academic lives if the opportunity presented itself in a pale hue. As I drifted around the college campus, I noticed the buildings were old, stoic and thick.

The first building I entered was the library. It was the tallest building on campus, a home for the wayward drenched in words. The entrance was welcoming. Wafts of ancient books gave up their scents. The moldy memories of history beckoning for all imprudent linguists to enter its fine majestic grip. The books smelt like aged skin hung from history's lamented arms. The entire building was like one giant grotesque woman who outlived her beauty and was reeling on the meagerness of the masses to continuously erect for her an overly venturesome facade, a scholastic siren made to wheedle the freshman class of their nostalgia.

Upon entering the library, I felt vaguely like a monk ameliorated and rejoicing on his past self-immolations. I wandered along the end of a long row of books in the literature section, a row of stories from sleeping people who once rode the world on magical balloons filled with the air of nonsense and ambiguity and who finally ended their journey in this twenty-story coffin. Writers, disregarded men of words, filled brittle pages with raw facts and abortive reasons. The pedantic troth feeds the minds of mice men as their deaths, both symbolic and tragic, become fodder for future rodents. A learned and stilted foundation formed from a figurative bed of stainless scholarly needles. The succulent blood spilling from those daring enough to sprawl on this bed of prickly needles, those unfortunates who place pen to paper, will in turn become the dust for another century's past.

The author's abandoned memories become staggered revenants promenading the library rows in college towns, immune to nostalgia. The library's beguiling body was vacant, lonely, and barren of fraudulent prestige. The gods of my greenness were dead decaying shores littered with tidal waves thundering. This place was full of dead gods waiting to be exhumed by prying eyes and minds littered with canonical forgetfulness.

I picked out six or seven books at random and read pages randomly from each to create a new dialogue between the authors. The authors spoke tangled sentences in different tongues, eluding remorselessly to some greater significance beyond weary words. When read together undiluted, some meaningful nothingness is garnered from the spectrum of words and phrases sung from different periods in different cultures with different clothes worn by devout peasants and kings wedded to virgin queens.

There is a sorcerous exaltation attained in the company of sleepy wordsmiths conjuring darkly eminent states of being from mere verbiage. Time is furiously cruel to writers. The spectral clock feeds them glorious thoughts of being consumed alive while its dreary talons dispassionately dig into their hearts to rid them of beating noises.

I found a lustrous self-hatred in the library of that college town. Never again would I want for a more delicate mouth with alluring lips to suck out the festering venom. I maintained and gloated over the literary poisons coursing through my bulging veins. When I left the library that day, I was resolved to die someday like old Mozart thrown into a bleak popper's grave unnamed and full of music.

There are occasions when sheer loneliness drags you so low you can barely reach up from the hell you're engulfed in to grab for the bottom of your freshly dug grave. We expect sympathy at the lowest hours but find the frigid ground just as unforgiving. If only it were possible to reach some evolved status, to hoard vacant states of hope until the physicality of being implodes. It was still possible to bring forth fanciful fairy tales, if only the horrid fates and their maniacal finger pointing fingers no longer wished to dine on my disintegrating corpse still ambulating.

Could I lead a different life, one of merriment and simplicity? Possibly. It would not be this day though, and I feel my days are slowly winding down.

Nothing over the next few months would be as enter-taining as the dead days before evening's arrival. I petitioned Hurakan, the storm god, for a new vocabulary to blatantly awaken the upheaval taking place in my brain. I looked forward to someone calling me at four in the morning to tell me a tragedy occurred. Enunciating this to myself in my out of body voice was tumultuous, like speaking to an estranged acquaintance, one who visits wearing the whimsical thrill for life draped over shoulders, forked tongue dangling, then invites you to drink from flaunted fangs to see if the bitter poison strengthens one's tenacity to be vindictive.

There are many different ways of acceptance and just as many different ways to not accept anything at all. I set out to make lasting bedfellows with self-indulgence and self-humiliation. Shame can prove to be a tremendous monstrosity in the fading mirror until you indulge its every whim, until you allow everything civilized humanity determines unworthy of forgiveness, unwholesome and deleterious, entrance into the vast unraveling psyche. Take it upon yourself, you despondent vocalizers of fearlessness, to dive head-first into some new morose identity.

The house was mostly empty during the day, but at night, all the roommates gathered for infectious drinking and abusive substance taking, playing mad loud music, before announcing to the world that we were subconsciously unstable and dreadfully infected. The roommates invited languid repetitive conversations amongst ruinous guests regarding the sullen quality of lives inhumanely entertained on television dramas and pornography. Nothing remained long before the sounds of discontent, that brutish beast riding on the back of existence, devoured the stillness and forced all in attendance to howl.

Many an entire day was spent in local college bars drinking away the Promised Land. Inebriated places to find pity in the avocado eyes of those unqualified to become human beings. Smug sardonic places full of pin-thin pupils, cocaine-laced girls high on sexuality, and fading bartenders serving way too many intoxicated poets.

The barfly relationships established, those without longevity as their goal, were not suitable in times of utter loneliness. These were tormented relationships requiring only the seconds before and after consciousness descends deeply. Attempts to make sense of the nonsensical nature of being bar stool fodder was futile and lacked laughable merit. The preposterous and exquisiteness of drunken humor graced those of little stature. The truly afflicted, those poor miscreants roaming, know that very soon the Cimmerian shade would overwhelm them. Most nights we gathered at the college bar called the "Wraith Cellar," then to the nearest bar to continue the barrage of ill feelings we harbored toward civility. After several rounds and many flattering stab wounds to the chest, contorted cannonballs of discontent were flung from awful intoxicated throats. Any unfortunate barfly within proxy of our calamities became doused in surging absurdities.

One of the roommates was named Bedford. He was the most ill-contempt person calamity could have ever coughed up. We shared the same appetite for excess, but Bedford did it with such ease as to make one question whether he was the Buddha reincarnated in the shape on a drunken belly full of blasphemy.

After returning from the bar one night in an awful state of words redundant and ebullient, Bedford and I began a dialogue the likes of which only the crowning prince of nightfall could embrace. Conversations with Bedford were less like attempts to persuade the other and more like competitively tossing a bulky ball made of tar and hardhearted blackness at each other until the other surrendered in a non-climatic collapse. A bitter downfall indeed. As with all temporal states of defeat, envy for the prevailing winds, sickeningly brilliant when viewed from afar, breeds new life into the trudging for Sisyphus's stone. It seemed like an appropriate time to question Bedford regarding his being blatantly antithetical.

Bedford was not one to prance around typical academic mandates most college students secretly longed for; the need to excel with a superior apprehension for the heroic forms chiseled into the bedrock foundations of knowledge. The collegiate competence required of a consecrated nothingness mumbles inanely to impress no person in particular. I saddled next to Bedford on the steps of our house and said, "Bedford, you told me you've been attending school here for three unremarkable years, and felt you had nothing to share regarding the epistemology of knowing how little one can know."

Bedford evaluated the question with a goat's grimace. He spoke in cigarette smoke and said, "I will tell you the one thing I truly feel has enabled me to last as long as I have, but this knowledge is slow moving, so be on guard. To endure with the coldest of blood is the way to enlightenment in a world of blood suckers.

"One night at the bar, after many, many drinks, I brought a girl back to the house whom I was previously discussing the plight of noble men. She was nineteen. She was a freshman who completed her first semester. She was painfully naive and volatile. A spurious mockery could not exhaust all attempts to describe her apparent frigidity as being sexually misanthropic. Anyways, I told her I was a philosophy major reading the works of F. Nietzsche. She loved the way I said 'Nietzsche' with an exuberant draw as if I was conjuring up the perpet-ually damned.

"Without speaking for several moments, I perversely stared for several seconds at her chest, then looked into her far-flung eyes. I asked her to tell me what experience buried deep in her memory was the most grueling thing she had never shared with another. She was unsure what I was asking, so I meticulously illuminated my inquiry.

"I concocted a completely and utterly fabricated story. I shared with her a deepest, darkest secret, though not mine, and made her promise she would never tell another person as long as she lived. I created a story of such profound repugnant ugliness that even I wondered whether it could have in fact happened during one of my many, many alcohol-induced blackouts. Those horrendous life-affirming blackouts you awaken from to find you're morbidly dissimilar in stature and cannot grasp the blank emptiness which birthed you that morning.

"You have to be cautious how close to actuality you get with some odious people. If your story of lurid debauchery veers too near the edge of manufactured lunacy, you might mistake yourself for the town's bumbling buffoon. Always remember, I told her, the goal for any action taken is the sordid taste it leaves in the mouths of the motionless, this is the true nature of reciprocity. I allayed her licentious curiosity by gently placing the tip of my finger on her twitching nose. She awaited my every word.

"And so the story I told her went something like this. Some friends and I went to buy cocaine. When we arrived at the dealer's house, there were several besieged men surrounding a young girl writhing naked on the floor. She was completely out of her mind from smoking cocaine. She flagrantly committed every bodily act of lured deceitfulness asked of her. I became enthralled with her contorting faceless facial gestures and the punctilious specter of revulsion draped across her naked body.

"We purchased several grams of cocaine and were invited to stay, to relish the arrogance of the fear-drenched room. We did. I became dolefully enraged with each line of white powder snorted. Then came the emasculate derangement, the breathless madness bursting in my nasal passages.

"All the ego sickness and dried out sentimental sensations for the improbable overcame thoughts of gentility as nefarious words engorged my mouth and sweltered on my tongue like crackling bacon on a skillet blackened. I wanted to join in the macabre scene with the young distraught girl undressed and insanely wriggling. Hesitantly, I approached the group of men surrounding her.

"Without saying or hinting to my presence being unwanted, they allowed me full access to the languid loveless performance taking place. As empty words fell from my twitching mouth, the room became darker and darker. I kept asking over and over who her father was and did he know how little her nipples were.

"She stopped her flopping on the floor, came to me on bent knees and opened her mouth as if to beg for a piece of embrocated bread or sanctified murkiness or some narrative regarding decency and correctness, but I just laughed harder and with more disdain as she longed with longing hands searching my nether region. Without provocation, one of the men standing next to me reached into his coat pocket and pulled out a small revolver, then handed it to me. I took the weapon, then told the flopping girl to suck the bullets out the barrel until the back of her brain coats the surrounding walls.

"Without hesitation, or fear of consequence, I maneu-vered the pistol toward my crouch and placed the barrel of the gun into her mouth with my finger on the trigger, not knowing if the gun was even loaded. Her mouth imbibed the barrel. Her bewildered lips and coated tongue so effortlessly swallowed the gun metal gray. For some reason, I became insanely jealous of her girlish awkwardness. I wanted to squeeze the trigger. I wanted to unload the bullets. I imagined these acts of defiance would fill her full of the intractability and vacuity she longed for, so I did - click-click-click-click-click-click.

"After six clicks of the gun, I realized it was empty. The timid men around me donned themselves in masks carved out of the pure fright they ingested with each clink of the revolver. The gun was empty, but so was I and so was her mouth, though she barely seemed to notice my actions other than to wink at me in approval as I dropped my head. I handed the gun back with her sloppy saliva still dripping from the end of the barrel, then walked back to the table for another line of white-powdered absurdity."

I was not sure what Bedford's story was meant to entice. He obviously wanted me to enunciate a similar sounding secretive debauchery of my own, but I had not lived long enough nor felt the sluggishness a valiant death affords. Surrendering to one's stupendous appearance is both laborious and grinding to the uninitiated herdlings. To interject anything worthy of such a devilish dialogue with Bedford requires the willingness to walk blindly into bottomless pits.

Bedford's eyes slowly rolled back into his head as he continued his story, but before he began speaking, a hollow space in my chest became full and was never to be replaced with reluctance again. Never again would I demand dilapi-dated acknowledgments, nor history's perverse justifications for the sickening breath curdling up in my mouth upon regur-gitating a sliver of Socrates's hemlock. I would laugh internally while the other garden variety sheep remained in exile doing things only sheep comprehend. I believe either of these foundations, to know Bedford or not to know Bedford, would suffice.

Doubt provides much sustenance for trudging. Discern what is tangible in tales tinged with autumn's allure, those vulgar legends of heroic deaths in glorious colorations handed down from one generation to the next. Flowery fortune-telling announcements engraved on sour city walls regarding the coming of spring will fail to arouse fledglings hiding dormant under bed-shaped coffins.

A tiny burst of modesty, the pungent vomit I kept buried within, imbued my mouth. I did not want to interfere with the symphonic and sorcerous sounds of Bedford's parable, so I swallowed it without flinching. Bedford took a drag off his cigarette and continued.

"After recounting how we departed the house, leaving the dwindling girl with her ghosts, I told her I had never spoken of the incident to anyone. She was ripened by the idea that she too could candidly divulge her deep darkness without the hindrance of societal judgments or keen moral compasses to measure one's ethereal acumen. A sublime hurricane of depravity trudged inside her. This was a truth-telling vagrant girl in search of chaste lands to decimate with vulgarities cavernous in scope. A most triumphant pause entered my chest heaving because the silly girl believed every fictitious syllable of my story and was now willing to divulge some hidden horrors of her own.

"She suddenly removed her shirt. She asked me to scrutinize her perky quarter sized nipples before she began to unravel the details of her deepest darkest secret. Her nipples were less than perfect and one had a small hair growing from it."

This was Bedford. He had a genuine yet distorted disposition regarding his personality. It kept you vaguely unhinged in his presence. I never fully understood nor lauded him. He chose to never fully acknowledge his sheltered imperfections. Bedford was unlike those daunting dinner guests with their dumb glances of appeasement tossed about, all horrified by their own wilting ignorance, their obese laziness, their engorged bellies full of fate's ugly demeanor, and their utter lack of civil charm whilst standing before time-honored mirrors.

The unclothed noodlings of a woman in Bedford's company was fertile ground for him to apply his godawful craft. He resisted making slanderous comments at first, then vengefully unleashed the ruthless leviathan. Bedford was not always approachable, nor was he deceptive when speaking of his appreciation for what some might consider Mephistophelian.

We were the unsung heroes of a story God would not have approved of, but we defined ourselves as heroes for the simple fact that we were suffering and God was watching. Being unsound with flimsy thin skin, I questioned whether making such a rudimentary statement was the act of an unabashedly hideous man in boy form with gaping chest, perpetually heaving to scatter his dying testicular seeds along the brittle barren seas of history. So, the story continued and my thoughts went on and on without notice.

"Please, Bedford, continue." And he did. Bedford went on with the story sounding stoic and reserved.

"So she slowly worked herself closer toward me. Her breasts were out and she delighted in pressing them firmly against my face. She started to whisper something mumbling into my ear. The saucy temptress then released the verbal contents of her tormented stomach stuffed with deliciously deep dark secrets. She was flawlessly reeling. She told me she lived with her mother and stepfather. With a twisting melancholic disposition, she began the tall telling tale of her father dying from a drug overdose. The lifeless lump was found several days after his death by a homeless man walking down the alley behind the house where she grew up. He was already severely rotted and irreconcilable.

"When the police came, they were unsure whether it was a body or a pile of rubbish coated in dark autumn's decomposing leaves. Her stepfather tried to comfort her sadness but did so in such an undignified manner while she sat desolate in his truck watching the officers poke and prod her father's rummaged carcass. Sorrowfully seated on stepfather's unsettling lap, the irreverent beast tightly squeezed her in his arms before slowly dropping one hand between her quivering thighs, then to the waist area before easing fumbling fingers underneath cotton candy panties. Forcing ring and middle fingers into her looming crouch, he assuredly slipped one inside.

"At first," she said, "he brushed along the tiny hairs of my recently developed femininity, then steadily circled and stimulated my newly formed bulb with his ring finger. The thrashing fear of being seen mixed chaotically with my unripened flesh swelling in impure delight. I came ferociously for the first time as my father's zipped up body in a black demented bag was dragged across the yard.

"At first, she desperately pleaded with her step-father to cease his pestilent fingers bungling. Overwhelmed in biting anguish for the patriarchal cessation, she was unable to process her stepfather's sickly sexual maneuverings. She trudged through disconnected feelings of libidinous trepidation so excitingly demur while morally baking under an unrepentant sun.

"I became a vague reference point for her to unload such impious incestuousness and dribbling perversities. As I listened intently, a thought, exalted yet sublime, began splashing around in my skull like the waves produced by a terrified man drowning. I pictured myself kneeling at her mother's hospital bed, and right before she took her last breath, I would tenderly whisper into her ear the vile story of her daughter's shameless transgressions. The dying mother would know her husband's treachery. Tormented thoughts of appending death layered with the angst of kindred debauchery. Non-existence coexisting with adulterous sorrows. I would relay the details of this brutal act of sexual betrayal so mother may find the banality of hell rewarding upon entering its wretched gates.

"She started to cry hysterically after the full weight of her story fell forlorn upon her shoulders. A wallowing wail of sorrow strikingly splintered her frowning face. I was so insanely aroused by her brazenly self-deprecating torments that I prematurely came unaided in my gray khakis.

"She then took off her pants and lace panties. A huge bulge of musty pubic hair filled her lap. She took my hand and violently rammed it into her crotch with such force it nearly broke my right index finger. My stumbling fingers became tangled in the murky mess. Her throbbing hairy hump was saturated in a tacky wetness which coated the golden glistening hairs of her nether region. The mop of pudendum hair was amazingly perpendicular. They ascended through my flailing fingers as if ascending toward God coming down to consecrate them like meager sinners hell-bent in their search for a dignified state of forgiveness."

"It's okay. It was always okay," she said.

Bedford looked at me as if doubting whether or not I was still engaged. He broodingly ended the demented tale of deeply disconcerting sexual encounters. To alarm Bedford's libidinal prowess with hints of underappreciation proved disastrous to many a wayward freshman maiden. To avoid any senseless provocations from Bedford, I moved not a single muscle on my face until I finally sneezed.

The inner faculties reflect on what the outside world of sorrows was swallowing. Being remote, far-flung and inaccessible, waves of finely coddled sadness permeated the melting caustic core of my being. I was overwhelmed with a magnificent thirstiness to never make sense of anything again upon hearing Bedford's unsettling yarn. The elusive pounding heart of mankind turns rusty in time like an old Cadillac parked behind some dead swamp.

How could I ever lean too far toward cruel unripened places in my belfry of a brain after having heard Bedford's snappy narrative of such fragrantly blemished humanness? I became lusterless. With a murky transparency, I would, henceforth, present myself as one who denies everything pithy and overtly moralistic to a submerged audience of plastic puppet people. With a slight hint of acceptance, I nodded to Bedford and nothing else mattered.

How could I possibly entertain a meager life withdrawn after having heard these two salacious stories? These word induced spectacles manifesting mankind's inhumanity toward fellow creatures, those cognizant cretans ambulating on hind legs? "Did you violate her, Bedford? Did she crawl away like a crippled dog after you motioned for her to leave? What happened after she removed her skin?"

We were both exhausted from the intensity of language. The drunkenness wore us down. Years later, I attempted to stage the same maddening thought experiment on a girl I became involved with after a three-day binge of alcohol and cocaine. I tailored the scenes to my own liking; the house was an apartment and the gun went off. Unfortunately, the girl housed nothing remotely dreary inside her formless figure. She tossed a spiteful smirk at my face, as if she heard this story before, then walked out without even asking if the gun painted the dull room a bloody-spattered brain color.

The next morning, I decided it was time to find some menial employment. I needed some financial resources to afford rent and my ever-expanding drinking and drug habits.

Food always seemed like an unavoidable option. I wandered through the unraveling downtown streets of a great western collegiate town in search of a help wanted sign.

A small art gallery near the campus was looking to hire a part-time staff person to help set up shows, man the entrance during the shows and repair and paint the walls after the shows were torn down. It did not pay much. They hired me on the spot.

The gallery owner was a heavy-set man who draped his huge torso in African-colored clothing. His name was Vidar. He garnished his mouth with an over-sized mustache. Crumbs of food and tiny limbs always dangled from it. Vidar barely got up from his desk because of the constant discomfort his weight caused on his knees. Instead, he pushed a buzzer on his phone when he wanted a staff person to get his coffee. The first time I answered the buzzer, Vidar told me to go next door and refill his coffee. I did.

I warily returned with Vidar's scalding libation. I wanted to toss the searing hot coffee onto his corpulent face to watch his mustache mollify in a caffeinated glow. The next time he moaned for me to get his coffee, I paused before telling him I would not lower myself. To demand the sick servitude of another was itself a degrading demonstration on Vidar's part, but to carry on like a gluttonous mess rumbling orders for trivial chores to fetching dogs with such a patronizing display was beyond all reproach. I was not going to fetch the morning paper nor was I going to make it any easier on Vidar's wilting wobbly knees.

Vidar had every right to fire me, but he surveyed my stance for a second, then told me to make some copies of some papers he quickly thrust toward me. Vidar's actions were those of a vain murderer who asked of his victims to dig out the knife he planted in their bellies so he could stab them again. He never asked another staff member to get his coffee, and those poor wobbled knees of his truly paid the price. I grew to like him very much.

Some days, when work was slow and Vidar was not busy, I sat attentively in his office learning about art and the history of art and its historical relevance to the African community, Vidar's area of expertise. I sat glued to his every word, wanting to learn more about the masks people wore while dancing around fires to entice the shaman's sleeping mind to renew the tribe with a burst of rain or meat from the hunt or ripened birthing loins to replenish the tribe's livestock.

The first day laboring at the gallery, I met a staff member named Elise. She was exceptionally full of melodramatic charm. Elise was abundantly mad with moxie for having emerged into the fractured world a distressed swollen offspring infected with the hopeless disease.

Never underestimate the extraordinary urges of women woefully unwanted nor the whys some deserving women rely on when the smiles of men become less than substantial. The provocative glares of unhealthy gentlemen pass mute before their once scenic reservoir of womanhood. Elise did not possess an absorbing preoccupation with others in general. She hated her blooming body because it was much larger than acceptable to the cosmopolitan worlds of window-shopping women. Elise tortured and tormented herself by plowing thru endless allurement magazines designed to make corporately that which the frowning gods intended to be glorified and worshiped. She spoke of the feminine models littering glamorized pages similar to the way elders venerated golden guardians satiating the masses with a stare. Elise sanctified the models' makeup induced faces with her solemn allegiance to never be beautiful.

Elise chose to inhabit the exclusive fantasies cosmopolitan type ladies magazines offered. To fathom the grueling ugliness she experienced within when making loathsome comparisons, those empty-vessel type comparisons, Elise would shun the full view of the mirror. The sanctified fashionistas cluttering the dull lifeless pages glared back at her with utter contempt. The countenance of radiant women who never aged was all the rage. And for Elise, the immortality of their appearance was a pestilent infatuation more formidable than the sting of an early grave.

Unexpected conversations followed Elise when she entered a room. She loved to talk about performing oral sex on the hurried men she met while trudging through downtown streets at night. Drunk on red wine, wearing thick lipstick lips, she drew into her mouth the most eager of men like a Venus-flytrap without the death thing once you entered her sticky grasp. Elise's eyes filled with unmitigated satisfaction whilst basking in blowjob memories. Once she identified the other as being horribly misplaced, vaguely familiar, yet sorrowful engorged, nothing could prevent the onslaught of poking prodding gestures emanating from behind her eyeholes. Something akin to the way a homesick dog looks while wagging its tail in front of a fiery flame shrouded house about to collapse and fiercely expire.

I thought it odd Elise never allowed anyone to take her picture. She was repulsed by her likeness and never wanted to lose control of it. Elise cursed the thought of her photograph, her lurid image, being taken by insincere men who, she imagined, would use it as a vicious tool for masturbation. Awkwardness was a blissful quality we shared. Optimism for a flowery future was a quality we despised.

I worked at the gallery every day for the next several weeks from early in the morning until mid-afternoon. After work, Elise and I would slush our way through dim bars we agreed were places least likely to be attended by anyone with a hint of dignity. Places filled with attendees so dreadful on the inside the bleak bar aroma, thickened by desolate drunkards breathing, revealed the vacantness of life. We found this barfly attribute delightful. The inhumane way a drunkard's lament is simultaneously attractive for merely having eroding flesh to flaunt, yet sensually repulsive for having the gall to wear it.

Elise's mocking appearance reminded me of a fragile girl, or a banished woman, tossed aside by the languid ladies she adored. She defined without cause the sunken mouths and drooping cheeks of femmes in need of an evening meal. In time, Elise's pessimism evolved from a vile bantering to a besieged vernacular lampooning optimistic nonsense. She vilified the exposed sensations of a pale mentality, the fawning sentimentality of the herd, and the overindulgence in authenticity while at the same time birthing a spectacle of fear for an otherworldly lonesomeness.

We were friends without reservations. We enacted all the chemically induced contortions. Every drug, whether uplifting or downtrodden, was devoured ruthlessly, and we did so into the wee hours, for days on end, while less than adventurous types fell to the wayside. We talked aimlessly over spurious things. Elise eloquently expressed the debauched with more veracity than the dry conversations held around us by all the damaged puppets and their legions of puppeteers.

When the gallery job was nearing its completion due to summer break at the college, Elise asked me to move in with her at the house her parents rented. It was out of a twisted sense of kindness mixed with loneliness on her part that she asked. A solemn offer, an intention-filled gesture no other person on this unbearable earth has ever replicated. I told my roommates, specifically Andre and Bedford, I was moving out and to freely rent my room to the next unwitting traveler.

They understood my departure without the need for long drawn out explanations. They were never friends with flimsy borders. These were not pulsating people lasting till the end of a protracted series of ego deaths and childlike rebirths after the great war within ends. The three of us once talked about the possible future, then began to hate each other for no apparent reason.

I moved into Elise's house and began insatiably reading books on French poetry, analytical philosophy and serial-killer biographies. I devoured them in six-hour spurts. Drifting into a midday literature-induced comas, into the haze of erudite ambiguity, I felt remarkably alive. The days passed. The nights were young and full of agony.

The fallacious and malicious were more important bedfellows to us than the innumerable boars who spent their dry academic days making stout points regarding certainty. The deviling mouths of the unlearned with their portly pretenses masquerading as eloquent verbiage. I lingered for hours staring out the second-floor window of Elise's room watching hookers across the street searching for a plague to unleash onto the world. Enacting venereal vengeance on the men who paid for their carnal misery. Tossed about on callous sidewalks until they're left for gutter deaths with the bitter taste of mankind's deary seed in their mouth. If only I had the resources to purchase all of them, then send them to foreign lands with foreign sands where lamentable time could not reach their aging allure, but I was poor and alone, and God hated me.

There are days so trying you can barely scrape them from broken shoulders. Those sinister days of condemnation hidden in heartless evenings. I awoke daily to find my nightmares were dribbling things with tempting fangs. Horrific apparitions cemented into the mind like freshly laid sidewalks on which forgotten children wrote their names and fowl words, endless streams of quickening reminders warning of things hidden and forbidden.

No matter how awful I felt at daybreak, I howled like a dying whore when evening's purple curse arrived. Elise always reminded me that today was fleeting, and tomorrow was fictional and to never expect any real connections with unraveling realities. Elise was a purple witch who conjured depraved spirits to watch as we dauntlessly ingested a myriad of numbing potions from the skulls of the reluctantly departed. Withered from being audaciously attentive to things besieging, we stumbled about like abandoned tadpoles rambling through littered streams, bodies eviscerated from the abundance of cruelty incessantly dropped from above.

Elise's vile attempts to catch me from falling down the stairs became a constant affair. How I wanted to feel the dreadful thud at the bottom. The bottom of unbridled audacity. The bottom of unmanageable desperation. A place known to cure the figuratively disturbed.

I sought aimlessly to find the serenity of servitude, longed diligently to covet corpulent families with screaming babies, to then die alone from a cold cancer-laded life. I glorified the smug reassurance of doom. The timeworn tribulations insane drifters conjured to curse fellow travelers were welcoming beacons to those who fear little. When things became too much, when thoroughly nauseated from the distinct taste of ephemeral bliss before the fall, when the wings of wax melted under the unconcerned sun, Elise would remind me that it did not matter, nothing was ever going to change the downward trajectory of a man as he slowly decomposes above ground.

Elise's words became grossly emancipating to those clinging to doubt. The trembling days and barren nights spent coddling regrets for neglecting things living no longer held sway over my dwindling imagination. Her alleviating words were an eerie outlet of sorts. Elise's roaming vernacular, when in the company of bleak faces attached to barren heads throttled, morphed into something immensely visual like grotesque postcards with pictures of back-alley cats shot up and served on plates of lettuce all dumbfounded. "Never on the road, but under the road," she announced. The ruinous steps of fate repetitiously trudged over the grimaced lives of all ugly humans with frightful delight, but the eyes of Elise, surveying and valuating, existed beyond all ticking clocks.

Tumbling through inescapable nights alone, when daylight burdens me no more, I reminisce about the time I kissed Elise. We were so heavily intoxicated and her lips glistened like crispy bacon. The urge came over me for no apparent reason. I told Elise I desired her mouth. The way she enunciated words, trenchant and deadly, like thorns puncturing the head of Christ crucified aroused the sinister in me. Elise leaned into my face and kissed me softly, then told me my breath smelled like old glue. We drank that night as if heaven was burning down all around us.

Awakened by morning's repugnant tug, the crisp autumn air enveloped my hungover body broken into millions of awful pieces on the front lawn. Clothing drenched in the aroma of cheap beer soaked in urine. Outstretched and face down in the middle of the yard like a wobbly intoxicated walrus with a book about robots in my right hand and in my left hand was a clump of brown hair.

How could this have happened again? Had the immutable bosom of non-existence beckoned me to slumber in her noxious grasp? A dry sense of obliviousness settled in the back of my brain as the blackout monstrosity gripped my tattered body. Swirling sorrows. Absurd premonitions. The gaping grave of yesterday hurriedly sought to swallow my fragile bones for the things I could not remember having done. "Give me a moment to get myself together," I howled at the grave digger. I hoped my request would buy me some time to arise, but I never did make my way from the metaphoric ground. This made all the difference.

Some wayward wanderer strolling by should have poured lye on the depleted lump of dubiousness passed out on the lawn. Piles of rotting pig flesh should also encompass the sickening mess. A wretched person surrounded in the slow decaying flesh of swine. I made my way inside the house and into the shower. My hands were shaking terribly, but I never let go of the book on robots. I threw the handful of brown hair into the toilet, then flushed it while shrugging as it rolled around the bowl.

Life becomes something indistinguishable when held a little out of reach. When the quietus overcomes my spirit to survive, and a deceitful state of mourning takes flight in my disordered mind, nothing more is required than the artful face of Elise to allay fears of unwinnable endeavors. Tragically, Elise died of pneumonia in her adult years. Consumed with unrest, I never bothered to find out how she was doing since we last spoke many years ago. She was a problematic girl. Elise was a twisted vestal sister who genuinely harbored my senselessness. A burgeoning blister worn down over time until she dimly burst without anyone noticing.

Shamefully, I fumble for uninhibited non-redactable diction to describe the lonesome subsistence we shared long ago. I am terribly aware of the end of language and the sullen charm of forgetfulness. When timorously overwhelmed with feelings of utter incompleteness, I solemnly wish to reach into the immense flaming death void and grab Elise's hand, as she so often grabbed for mine whilst falling down those deplorable stairs, to profess my desire to get lost with her in all the ugly bars, in all the underworlds, while consuming glorious gallons of self-destructive brews till the sun turns black as sackcloth.

The suspicious poets declare life to be cruel like prepubescent boys dubiously taking hold of their dangling member for the first time wondering whether to stroke it to completion or just cut the damn withering vine off before the deep damage becomes irreparable. Elise, I cannot wait to suffer death just to see you again. But for now, I must continue to write this story, this thing that grows in me like a sadistic testament, while you remain decomposing food for hungry worms in a graveyard no one enters. The maggots plagued your eyes and your hands rotted so lonely without me, Elise.

That being said, I digress. I trudge a little slower back into haunted memories because the surrounding air suffers without words. A tale of unraveling awfulness continues.

When the overall sense of self, the ability to know thyself and the fortitude to resurrect one's dead self, is merely a shadow thrown by falsifing phantoms loitering across the windowpanes one gazes out in fear of approaching strangers, the bruised vanity of daylight seems trivial. Gazing out familiar windowpanes as a young maelstrom, stumbling and stammering for new air to inhale, I devolved into this grief-stricken creature with incurable and unraveling sorrows swelling in the stomach. I was confused. The empty words and sensationalized images counted on to provide the centrifugal centering force to even wheeze consistently dissipated like dawn's unwelcomed dew.

As months past, Elise and I met many kindred souls, groups of throbbing people, many of whom became engendering friends going off similar saneness rails. Murky individuals who wore long and eager fangs and partook in the same self-indulgent behaviors designed to elicit distress. We were the prodigiously hidden generation. A vile generation of the most similar shortsighted thinkers aimlessly gathered together on piles of disappointment's debris. Searing dissatisfaction for everything bland piled upon the enchanting devil-tries of casual sex, designer drugs, and things blatantly unavoidable to the sickened traveler, defined and molded the character defects of this milk feed generation. A mixed bag of idly slacking disrupters breeding with cynical social inter-rupters, both questioning western civilization's watered-down ideals.

It was then I met Seane. A non-practicing apostate with a furious predilection for sorcerous substances of all kinds and quantities. He could also secure a plethora of conscience extinguishing chemicals. Seane's simmering clairvoyance, when nestled near, grasped the deficiencies existence presented, then reshuffled the comical cadence of living till time tottered atop the high wire unaware of the unforgiving ground. Seane was my towering twin. In time, he became Elise's furious lover at the expense of all that was abnormally normal.

I met Seane one night while entering another blackout abyss alone on a bar stool. He sat next to me, then surveyed the inebriated landscape for fertile felines. He was all smiles and talked in endless riddles like a schizophrenic monk meditating out loud. In a heavy drunk, most words lose their jagged texture and become mumbling buffoonery before taking flight on the backs of nonsense swirling.

Seane was attending classes at the college and was glad to hear I was not. After conversing for an hour over redundant small talk gibberish and plotless stories about nothing, I asked if he knew where to find something virulent to inhale, something sickening to ingest, or anything vulgar to the tongue.

"I am not sure you could even get off the bar stool, let alone smoke deleterious things," he said.

"You do not know me, but the unraveling distance between the unpleasantness I am trying to banish with drink, and suffering the next laughing stranger's putrid face existing within fractions of inches of my dried-up cunt of a life, has motivated me on many a dark eve to be thoroughly infested," said I.

An unusually agreeable sensation coddles drunkards completely unaware of anything that happened the prior evening. The distilled preoccupation with memory eviscerated. Any and every attempt to bring to the surface frayed recollections swimming in gross libations is futile and utterly hopeless. Heedfulness ceased upon regurgitating all the booze and late-night bar food. Tormenting time swallows the intoxicated soul before solemnly sauntering the drunken bones to diseased floors. The next morning would be no different. One in a long series of dreadful mornings to never remember, but that particular morning was tinged with a slight hint of voodoo in the air. Seane and I found the forgetful poison, indulged, then trudged home in blurs becoming blurrier. Apparently, Seane stayed long before passing out on the living room couch.

Seane and I formed an amicable alliance. A singular reassurance garnered from having a sociable seraph to defend against calamitous details, like the demanding hand of Jehovah thwarting aside iniquitous things creeping down slaughtered suburban streets, was given its due. A generous friendship formed from descending downward spirals never divulged, the looming murkiness wallowing within, and the calm scent of sea snakes boiling became our agreed upon stature. Since the death of Mark, I slipped remotely adrift regarding close male acquaintances, but that all changed with Seane.

Seane was a man who believed in things being together. Numerous ladies lingered around his steps waiting for plentiful portions to sedate their shivering loins. Seane never capitulated to senseless trembling. The outdated narratives used to describe or enact vague metaphors to explain a man's character were painfully useless with regards to Seane. The use of context to frame an authentic person billowing fails time and again because the generic person, the lewd model strutting before its unhappy creator, lacks the nuances audacious characters portray in public and in private.

When near them, those defiantly grotesque spectras, fearless to a fault, singled out from the blameless herd and draped in ethereal drippings, and a tiny flake of piety lands on your wary shoulders, you are afforded the realization that not a single shuddering soliloquy could compete with mankind's dystopian charm. There is no pretension in the hands. No dried-up vestments draped across dauntless shoulders. There is wisdom without the need for certainty like truth without the giver of lies. Not long thereafter, Elise and I both agreed Seane should live with us. We asked Seane, he agreed, then we all drank like the infuriated children of Bacchus being torn to pieces in celebration of the coming finality.

Evenings proceeded in drunken blurs followed by lonely sunrises woolgathering. Still coddling the ridiculous notion of a better life, a vague awareness regarding the folly of serious fashioned footsteps ambulating down prosperous streets began to prey upon my fragility. Does an imposing matrimonial presence in life secure a hallowed pause in the unhappy heart of a man walking with foreign feet fashioned from the clay of prosperity? A nonchalant woman with few if any morals not minding the monstrous mystery unraveling. Am I to pensively scrutinize the dimly lit eternity to discover a beautiful swine to bear the company of shadows with during banal and disheartened times, those old-age nursing home matrimony days which mask the ever-growing senselessness one inherits simply by being a rotting to death thing?

It was not difficult to see the libidinous gestures Elise casually tossed toward Seane. She lived in his footsteps and did so with admirable dignity. He appreciated her intimate kindness and held onto her hand softly after debauched outsiders lumbered home at days end. The three of us would drift along abandoned dialogues, weigh the weight of the world with words, gather up the appallingly imminent signs encircling us, and disregard the unconventionality of silence in the face of a dying world.

"Is there a single thing, a spike or stone, you wish to subdue before confronting your darkest day?" I said festively. The room was quiet. Elise spoke first.

"I prefer I go blind. I do not want to be afraid of the all-encompassing blankness before I enter it, before I am one in being with the unrelenting void."

With a puzzling glance at Elise, Seane said, "I want to see before I see no more. I want to know the end of edification is near, and when it does bedevil me, I will then go sightless. No more tunnels unraveling. No more lights flicking at the end.

"My mother once told me about a friend of hers who was in a terrible car accident. The woman's face went through the front window before being thrown from the car. She did not die immediately. The poor woman lingered on for three agonizing days until finally dying a cold hospital corpse. Before she died, though, my mother visited her. My mother tried to remain expressionless when she greeted her dying friend, but the sadness was just too painful for her to bear.

"Tormented and defiled from anguish and agony, the dying women spoke with a withering tongue. Fading words wandered slowly from her mouth due to medications she was given to ease the damage done. The ebbing woman waved her fingers gesturing for my mother to come to the bedside. My mother approached her side, leaned down, and placed her ear near the woman's mouth to hear what words such suffering birthed.

"The woman lacerated face told my mother she was not afraid to die, and in a moment of clarity, she told my mother it would be much worse to continue living. She wanted my mother to know her life was horrible. Death was a welcomed face and to not wallow in prolonged sadness. Such nearsightedness is often mistaken for authentic honesty when there was no longer a need to be authentic nor honest."

"Can you imagine the unraveling sorrows? The pending loss of self she was about to experience?" said Elise. I was not sure whom Elise was speaking of, the mother or the dying woman.

"My mother was not her dearest friend. If anything, they were strangers similar to the members of this household. Strangers stranded on the same twisting rock imagining the wretchedness desperately hidden in isolation will remain buried. We only speak of sincere pain when bound up in concealment. The burgeoning neurotics, those stoic western souls, enrich psychiatrists for maintaining the code of silence and their willingness to listen attentively while hidden horrors are expressed. Can either of you recall telling anyone how awful they were? Have you ever divulged horrible thoughts harbored horrendously within to gain some access to higher states of psychological satiation?" said Seane before laughing abruptly.

Without flinching, I said, "As a matter of fact, I do. Disengaged abominations tormenting sunken eyes, senseless shame slumped over mangled shoulders, rampant remorse incessantly heckling within the paranoid head, and things uttered obtusely while in a drugged state of perfect madness, were not foreign foes."

They looked at me as if I turned an obdurate green whilst the horns of Beelzebub burst from my forehead. I explained Bedford's game of divulging the darkest secrets glistening deep within. I discussed the plurality of formidable pleasures dauntlessly dined upon with tattered women drooling. To nonchalantly confess bitter sorrows spiraling for having acted maliciously in general, was to no avail. Struggling with demented debauchery for an uncluttered voice to give song to slippery indiscretions and obsessing over the mounting inattention given to things scatological was not the type of operatic nonsense Elsie nor Seane found interesting. I ventured despairingly with guarded abandonment as the conversation turned forever fruitless.

"Then tell us what it was. What deeply dark abominations have you experienced? What roving wretchedness is hidden within," Seane said.

I comically discussed the drugged girl and the imaginary gun I injected into her begging mouth, how the damaging effects of hope belabored me, and how the sickeningly grinning girl then begged me to load the weapon with real bullets to send her home in a final box. Lies and more callous lies fell from my mouth like sour blood-tinged vomit one pours forth onto dingy alehouse floors once the venomous fangs of remorse bloat the belly. Whether they believed me or not, I do not know.

There is nothing so profoundly depraved as a fallen man claiming to have committed things contemptible and repugnant. They expect others told these tortured tales, heinously distasteful stories of cocaine sins, unbounded lust enacted and gun barrels emptied, to remain unwavering while sitting aloof. The mongrels of bewitched reasoning trample foolishly warmhearted folks before carving up their Weltan- schauung for pleasure. With words sharp like arrow tips to pierce the unexpected, the unguarded chest heaving, my feeble voice swiftly shuddered before Elise and Seane's unapproving eyes.

There is a tendency to mock dreadful voices enamored. A weakened whisperer in the ear is cursed for demonstrating the gruesome valor and remorseless grit required to birth such abhorrent stories. Is it not mankind's all-consuming brain, that infuriating instrument, which comprehends as it thoroughly inflames the dark wellspring of humor? A shamed stooge jesting to an exasperated audience of familiar people longing for acceptance, yearning for acknowledgment at the fleeting end, was met with fitting jeers to remove myself from the doomed stage of civility.

When the tangibility of becoming one of those tender personages addicted to anything contemptible, abominable or generally repugnant, one who mainlines culturally banned notions into the body and becomes engorged, tricked and palpably poked, a wayward man whose lonesome bones have neither home nor nourishment immaculately grasps the definitive meaning of disgraceful differentiation. Have we mislaid the power to control our background narratives? Shall we vindictively dine from the plates of lesser hopeless shadows? Were they not served a grim reality? Imbeciles lacking the genuineness of a mental harbinger recede into their own rotting souls. Unable to stand erect whilst spit on repetitively by a miniature army of factual devils and boring soothsayers, the monsters of manners gather together in fear of approaching tomorrows. Fathom thyself to uncover some antiquated apology for hollowed-out revelations as the wintering sun of life droops and awakens the shrinking possibility of another dark era within. To know thyself is as absurd as being a pale flaccid object lambasted by a deaf-mute ghoul.

Elise and I were unearthed from the same toxic sludge. Fashioned from the same polluted sands of time. When Seane entered our lives, we became more sequestered and less amiable to each other. Elise and Seane wanted alone time. They wanted to be insulated from me. Without my presence was the dagger dripping. Enunciating this notion of mine, that their secluding themselves was a vile proscription on their part to propel me further down the mercurial rathole, to force me back into the lethargic tomb of a life, was met with apathetic disregards. It was stillborn before it even entered the dead air surrounding their dead ears.

There is a dreadful silence in the world within. Too many memories to expound upon. The maniacally thin veneer of reassurance provided, either willingly or ceremoniously, is not a well-chosen defense against secular snares, and its shrinkage, under the weight of time's unholy grip, has become more and more apparent. I was not with Elise and Seane as I was with Mark and Cindy. I was a lingering abandonment in their company. An unappreciated mess of a man clearly defined by absence and not fulfillment. As absurdly blameless as anything awful ingested over time, I took to places where shadows devour enlightenment. Metamorphosed into a musty penumbra hung in the room no one enters. An annoying umbrage silently twisting in the room where the raven dreams.

I was working one day at the art gallery when Elise told me. Apparently, my lewd and unsound behaviors as of late were effecting the her overall mood. Elise thought I should find a new place to reside. Though I did not disagree with her ruling, it still stung in places kindness does not follow. After drinking more alcoholic beverages than should be allotted to one person, I crawled home on all fours that evening. Intoxicated and with much false gusto, I swung through the front door of the house on a vine of misguided vindictiveness before the coming collapse gathered me from the floor and poured me into my room.

The emerging darkness guided my every step. I went to my room, locked the door, played John Coltrane's "My

Favorite Things" as loud and disrespectfully as possible, then took an entire bottle of sleeping pills purchased earlier that day along with a bottle of Chianti and several red candles. The white pills were arranged into a generic smiling face on the floor. I lit the red candles. The Chianti was tasty and cold. With each pill swallowed, I defiantly howled, "I am the damned thing in the damned world."

The inscrutable darkness did indeed follow. It did not take long to pass out. But before doing so, I studied the remaining shivering leaves of autumn on a tiny tree outside my window. The leaves were calmly dying due to winter's encroaching kiss. How fitting it is to find that isolated loneliness for life on the branches of a timid tree beneath me. A direful acceptance of the coming harvest enveloped me. The wicked reaped before the fall. The chaff separated from the seed. The ugly gods gather the fallen flock before ushering them into the lusterless ground. Emptied of exaltation, the ebbing one counts each breath as they quietly pass. They will be the last. So comforting is death when it comes at an hour of one's choosing.

Needless to say, I traveled auspiciously into the blank blackness of non-existence before the doctor's penlight flickered across my eyes. A jolt of sentient light filtered through the profound blankness and provoked a sudden reaffirmation in my lower mammalian brain. I was once again in the land of the horribly reanimated and devalued masses. The slim possibility of being reincarnated, born beguiled again in the body of a bluebird, quickly dissipated. I could not understand a single thing spoken by the white garments wobbling around me. They filled my throat with tubes to suck out the sleeping pills, the unforgiving booze, and all remaining hope. An unsettling creation crawled back into being. Forlorn death waited patiently in the car. It left the motor running.

My arms and legs were bound to the table. I was duplicating. I was hallucinating. I saw dark-brown and white colored owls, large as bales of hay, flying around the bed. When I acknowledged their presence, they would dive like Apollo in flight toward my face before vanishing within inches of their prey.

This went on and on like a needless song brimming with ostentatious delights. A white garment entered my room and came near the bed. I tapped on the side of the bed with my hand motioning for her that I wanted to write something down to alert them. I was cognizant enough to question things going on. When she gave me a pencil and a pad of paper was placed near my hand, I scribbled the only word I could recall valuing - "Why?"

The nurse read the word, leaned down toward my face with a quizzical expression splattered in copious amounts of maquillage, then said, "you tried to untether yourself and you're in a hospital."

Life would never be quite the same again. Not that I was terrified of death, but its recourse would never again be so fundamental in my life choices. Daily understandings to determine dignified actions would not allow the meaningless of the present to persuade me again.

The foolishness of failing to end one's life cannot be understood with rambling words. The power to end a life of sorrow is simultaneously laudable and ludicrous. Having gone there, that demented place of self-extinction solutions, and to have returned barren of form, I witnessed the discordant glances of those aware of my destructive endeavor. The dread of life ending conspicuously thrives in every single living thing. The guiding fear lurking in man's ethos resides in the eyes. The awful awareness of soon being deceased. Beloved bedfellows willfully denying the doleful day their fruitless physicality too becomes compost for future dust storms of forgotten bygones is ripe with sentimentality. Callously passing judgment on those trudging oblivious through life, death's uninitiated masses prance about on hind legs stoically unaware of the dying day approaching.

There is a distinct and trembling dread mankind harbors. Others, other meager herdsmen and herdswomen, simultaneously beckon for one amongst their cursed lot to provide them a window into the otherworldly. These shrunken citizens stand in allegiance to a windswept flag, then drop to their knees to beg upon history's leg for scraps. Infectious tongues wagging for rewarding affirmations from obsolete masters. These are the diseased people trudging through history. They exist between the before and the coming immaculate coldness of dust. A livable death became them long ago and winds wicked and thorough blew their pious fingers asunder. The sorely noticed others, haunted kinsfolk floundering along with looks genuine, accurate, and heavily burdened from shouldering the injurious deeds of fattened forefathers, gather around dearly departed notions of sacrifice, civility, and the towering notion of shared responsibility, before settling into a good night's rest. The frowning members of the hospital staff gathered around the bed as if to shield the weary world from the exposed ambiguity pouring forth from my crippling emptiness.

They were experiencing obscene dreadfulness. A resounding quietus filled their eyes. They fumbled to gaze upon the mockery of my unmovable feast laying before them. Witnessing the glistening fragile letters inscribed upon my forehead by an otherworldly visitor –SUICIDAL, they averted their eyes in shame.

Slumbering for three days in the sleepless underworld, I wrestled with giant three headed alligators chomping and ten headed bats swirling before reentering the black hole to back home. Elise took it upon herself to contact my family, my mother to be precise. When the tubes were taken from my throat and I was able to speak again, my weeping mother entered the room like an unsought divining rod coming to rest before a hidden reservoir of sludge. The blotchy spectral owls haunting my room scattered as if a grim Hades heralded their return. Mother entered the hospital room one horrific day in November with hands icy and raw as they shook. She grasped my left hand neatly nestled under cotton bed covers.

Mother appeared utterly defeated from the sadness swelling in maternal recesses. So entirely removed from her once youthful tranquilities, mother had grown accustomed to being mournful on account of her son's enduring and detailed history of being abominable. The unfortunate few, mothers of melancholy minded sons, roam infertile grounds with wallowing shards of heartache harvested from the blackened fields of self-untethering broods.

What loathsome womb monster enraged and provoked such devilish and salacious urges in fragile fetus brains before flopping from mother's dapper flesh-tomb? Mother and I had not spoken in years. At first, I wondered whether or not it was mother standing at my bedside. Was it some beatific shroud draped before me like a dangling ghost? A hallowed manifestation of might to startle the recurring owls? The few words I attempted tumbled from my mouth like vomitus chunks of unripe bread. "Forgive me. You deserve not this lump of Christmas coal."

A fitting consolation is not something death benevolently grants. Nor does it provide grand affirmations for the cessation of life. The ruination of all things held dear swaddles generations of deceased dogs and towering kings alike. Time remains indifferent to the sorrows of man. When does the kind voice of appeasement, one born in the vacuum of time, arrive at the tiny ear of a tired woman exhausted from anticipating her nursling's more than prodigal ways to wither?

Mother never grasped the seriously alarming nature of her son's withering sense of self. What mother wants to bury her child below the merciless ground? Mothers are sanctified vengeance to an evil world of snakes. When mother entered the somber hospital room, held my hand, drove away the morphing owls massing, she achieved an anointed and exalted status amongst the unknown builders of men.

Not many men confront the starless face of nothingness and return. When they do, like the risen Lazarus, they are left to wonder what life will be like in the same village amongst the same people who recently buried the lifeless mess of a man. Can you begin to speculate how many questions the people surrounding Lazarus would ask over and over? "What is it like in hell, in heaven? Did you see the others trudging along the dusty streets of Jerusalem?" A chorus of earthly voices questioning the unquestionable as Lazarus walked the cobbled streets alone and impervious to the night caving in.

Tossed back into the discolored world without the clarity of Lazarus, I was saved from the bitter end by those who claim to worship the unraveling beginning. I recovered slowly after weeks spent swaddled in padded rooms with the same schizophrenic men who crawled through those biblical streets with Lazarus at their side. The bequests of insanity drags them on and on. They remain eternally alone with the rapacious fear of others gnawing away at whatever was left of their sanity. Vile self-recriminations and ever-expanding declarations of self-hatred pirouetted before my ever-fading semblance. The old dead me was forgotten by the awakened pulsating me. The passive bastard of the past was replaced by a demonic voice unfolding and a razor-tinged tongue for lashing.

When healthy enough to leave the other psych ward inmates with my theory of sanity being a myth created by rats to confuse all the wondering mice, Andre picked me up at the front of the hospital. I was still too coated with mind-suppressing chemicals to make a run for it, and Andre wore such a friendly smile I could not help myself but enter his car. Andre found a car, not an illegal one, so I could leave that lunatic fringe behind. Friends will find the time to remember those ill and in need.

No family came. I was not welcomed by either Elise or Seane. Not that I blamed them. Who would? The mentally distraught were not acknowledged in the towns of their birth, or so I am told. When I opened the car door and entered, Andre looked at my slightly riddled posture and said, "You finally look like a treacherous poet who forges lugubrious words from the depraved binges of a drunkard bent."

Maybe I was. I could only get a few words from my mouth. "And you look invincible. You look ginger and friendly. Should I devour your flesh or give you a gun to shoot me from afar?"

As we drove off, I watched the emergency sign above the hospital entrance fall from view and did not look back again, neither figuratively nor literally. I often give consideration to, as well as pay homage to, those fading afterthoughts, those debased ones still dressed down in hospital gowns. I left them all behind that doleful day in November's fury. Those inwardly unfortunates who could not come to grips with life's horrific fabrications, either before them or within them, remain confined like notes in a tower of tremoring song. They faintly mumble on evenings tossed about terribly intoxicated on the red of wine. Covered in hideous riddles, I hear them throbbing about unhinged in psychosis induced seclusion. Becoming quieter. Becoming manageable.

Trying to make sense out of what happened, to somehow characterize the feigning reality of bridges collapsing behind as the road before is veiled in tantalizing hues of forgetfulness, was impossible in the land of the living shadows. Destabilizing aberrations taunted my tomorrows. Unbeknownst thought catchers buried deep in the brain prevented the anti-psychotic chemicals coursing through my veins from reaching those hilarious places most chivalrous folks frown upon. Obscene notions of an unlivable existence, flopped from the loins of alienation and indifference, can be lasting bedfellows when life no longer calls out for neither candor nor compassion.

Andre took me back to the house we once shared. We were greeted by several old roommates still residing there. For some reason, they were all dressed in cherry-colored clothes from head to toe. Ironically, they shared many of the same insidious qualities as those I left cowering in padded rooms vacated of all aspirations. I did not stay long.

Without much thought, I withdrew the several thousand dollars I saved while working at the gallery, then wandered around aimlessly until I could walk no more. I wanted to be alone. I found a cheap motel on the edge of town, some depleted edifice to house my bristling exhaustion.

It was noon. The girl at the desk said they had a monthly rental available. I did not bother to ask how much it was, paid and went to the adjacent bar for a couple of beers, then a couple more.

My clothes were hacked from me by the paramedics. I did not have any anything to wear besides the jogging pants and tee shirt mother brought to the hospital. When I ventured back to my room, I laid naked on the bed and slept for weeks before deciding to reenter the outside. Nothing gained by entering life too soon. As the streetlights surrounded me, as the night owls fluttered above, as the frigid air of sensibleness became darkened with trivialities, fraught with lapses in befitting judgments, I quelled my steps before entering the encroaching drudge of another evening.

A disfigured girl, short of clothing, paused outside of a bar across the street from where I was standing. I decided to make her acquaintance, then find a common dialogue and entice her back to my room for some adult audacity to overwhelm the vile senses. She appeared to be devoid of righteousness. Being discreetly perverse, I watched as she softly rolled her luscious hips toward the unrelenting street, pacing back and forth under neon absurdities hunting for a formidable fix to ease her back into sanity.

I warily wobbled in her direction, but, before lascivious words even fell from my drooling mouth, the walking woman turned sickly blue, entered a stranger's overcast vehicle, then sped away. Impregnated with sanity's taunting demands, I regurgitated my evening meal all over the sidewalk. Conversations mattered little with the wayward women of my liking. Having lost all basic motor skills necessary for grown-up conversations once the vile substances took hold, there was nothing left that even mattered enough to converse with other doused souls. Nothing gave pause to the mounting voices of trepidation beckoning. I felt like a quivering bowl of gelatin dumped out for the deranged and the maniacal, those fearless street sweepers united, to scrape my grotesquely gummy self from the sidewalk's sadistic gripe. If only the star gods would usher in the rains to wash away my daunting remains down diabolical sewer drains.

Drunkenly stumbling back to the motel that night, two cops patrolling pulled alongside, jumped out with much intensity, then, with guns drawn, tossed me against the car door before placing me into the backseat. They refused to answer any of my questions. We drove to a liquor store near the motel where I was staying. As we approached the front of the liquor store, the cop in the passenger seat called the owner. The cop asked the owner to come and take a look, to identify the drunken man throbbing in the backseat. The owner took a peek and told the officer I was not the guy. The officers then drove me back to the motel without saying a word. As I existed the vehicle, the bloated cop apologized for the inconvenience.

Having an utter distrust and distaste for the entire authority apparatus, I sarcastically asked one of the officers for their station's phone number. I wanted to make a charitable donation to their annual asshole awards extravaganza. I assured both officers, they each deserved, with much adulation from all the rabid dogs foaming, to be awarded the highest of accolades for their selective memories and boring sentences. They were not happy with my assumptions regarding their authoritative leadership qualities nor their grammatical laziness. One of the officers tried to strike me, but I warned him I recently attempted to untether myself and would not be fooled by his poor attempts at manhood.

The bloated officer, though, drew back his bloated hand. The ridged hard hammer of punishment seething. Incorporating eons of law enforcement teachings, the despicable dog catchers adapted to the ways of man by eliciting fear within the silent herd.

Doubting dictates the servant class citizen's willingness to play victimization games. The trenchant rules define and determine the correct posture for the poorest of players. Untenable rules for the masses enshrined in, and enforced by, the tattered constitutions the corrupt classes cling too.

The maddening officer with his demented appetite for inflicting injustice was not aware of the look yet. The scrutinizing suicidal glare has been known to cause frigid minds to warily unravel. The unremitting thaw of being seen ignites dread in the hidden hands of authority's blue born soldiers. The piercing glare of lunacy can decimate entire worlds of lawmen. A timeworn tyranny created by authoritative crocodiles thrives in swamps unattended by curious minds.

The disquietude of punishment renders the wayward mute from a distance, but to truly catechize the congregation, the deed must be done snarling face to snarling face. Should one dread the inevitable, though nimbly disguised, state of dominance granted to a few at the expense of the many? I stood firm before the tower man with his towering blue ego. The other officer stepped in to separate us, instructed me to be on my way, then signaled the bloated office back into the police car. As they drove away, I thought about giant comets striking the earth.

We may distance ourselves from blatant cranial cravings for the slaughter, but the slaughter still arrives unavoidably in forms one could never have imagined. The destructive teachings of worldly antagonists the likes of which only macabre hellscapes could cough up are bound to our species like flight to the birds? Punishment's aim to overtake, to inhabit and counterbalance the headstrong immoralists residing in unreachable places, outlives its necessity once the mortal kings of carnage fall like lice from the earth spinning. Unfortunately, those who dwell long in unreachable places, the grand inquisitors who permit the cultivation and fertilization of the burgeoning erudite within, become their own reluctant prison guards in time.

The westernized caste system lacks all conviction for repairing the broken beings it delineates with fiery speeches and soaring soliloquies. Flaccid acknowledgments of hopefulness give affluence not to the feeble minds huddled under a firmament of chicanery but glorifies the less then citizens for their willingness to die under diseased blankets without moaning to loudly. Want not the protection of dying kingdoms! Opposed to the certainty of dying kings! Beware the security state of almighty seriousness! Inattention gives rise to the villain's gun. Blames the poor prostitutes and vagrant hordes. The flagellant designers of crime bestow guilt and shame on the burdened backs of indisposed men and women who suffocate, who hang in desperate surrender to the lionized lizard kings and their armies of godless dogs salivating.

The incredulous momentum to be nothing garnered before choosing to swallow a bottle of sleeping pills did not carry me far after returning to the waiting world of the somewhat sleeping. I was acquainted with Andre, Bedford, Elise and Seane. Was I not once shrouded by a complete sense of completeness, or wholesomeness, before the hallowed superego bruised the ugly anointed one within? Not in the slightest. To comb the ever-fawning distance between two vague points in time, gray amorphous places, aided only by staggering amounts of booze and illicit substances swirling, is a dauntless adventure for the maddening magnates indulging themselves in mendacity.

I did not recognize anyone anymore. It was definitely time to leave this place. The glue used to adhere myself was coming unglued. The sanctimonious serum spilling from my soul hole was prophecy unraveling. Some must believe before seeing. One must transmogrify. One must become monstrously abhorred. Become a doleful thing strangers endure patiently in long lines waiting for a chance, a turn, to manifest their hatred, to loathe and belittle your meager existence. What glorious vulgarity births such a hatred-baby into the modern minds of men and wandering monkeys?

Pedantically compelled, I set off for the campus library every day to read as much as able before being summoned by evening to slurp from the sorrowful well of unwell spirits. Nourished on foreboding strangeness, leather bound authors guided me toward baleful afflictions in need of hands and feet. When surrounded by those wretched bastards of academia, I felt wholly at home like a washed-up whale waiting for the sun to do its damage. The keepers of argument, with their proper veneer, never underestimate the unwillingness of the masses to learn what was being taught by the pedagogues they despised.

Apathetic students simply want passing grades to ensure their families financially float them thorough fun time academia, semesters upon semesters *ad nauseum*. Freshmen monkeys will feign interest in slightly gluttonous lecturers to fictitiously redeem themselves along the road to pure academic decadence. Completely and innately comfortable in the dank landscape of far-flung hyperbole, sorted and stacked on many library floors, I was without equal in my desire to cast out the ghosts of antiquity. "Prepare the cloth to be worn and the words to be spoken," I whispered to no one.

In a quick minute, my burgeoning usage of ravenous substances surpassed that of the general population of under-privileged rats. It would eventually eclipse my daily alcohol intake. There is a laboriousness in losing oneself to an immaculate-chemically induced chaos. Whether it be colorful pills, magic powders or plush green plants, when Rimbaud rocks you in his drunken boat and Baudelaire wheedles your blood from his bed of needles, you become rancid from the nausea of Sartre's other recoiling in your gut. The green fairy brew stews in the belly before being regurgitated on futile wastelands where women and their shadowy doppelgangers dance in ever expanding circles.

Deciding that enlightenment was a hoax and man really evolved from plants and not primates, I put my listless friends to task. On one unpleasant occasion, I visited Elise and Seane to see what became of my grueling afterbirth. They harmoniously hurled shameful curses at me for indulging in those sickly-sweet substances. Insisting it was having a massive hand in my downfall follies. They despised the devious chemicals I devoured frantically as if the fertile lands of sorrow would no longer provide the sad elixirs that wobble and make impure that which I pretended to be.

We talked about the nauseated people we befriended and the after-hours parties we attended. Without holding tightly to fading memories, our conversation avoided any direct reference to past succors to guarantee tomorrow's grinning glow remained elusive. Instead, dishonesty and inauthenticity held sway over our demented faces. I was a reluctant visitor to their evolving world of conjugal pleasantries. Morosely toting their sulky dislikes, I trudged toward the bathroom next to the room I once resided in, the room where the lingering ladies aroused me late into blank evenings to smoke copious amounts of pure Colombian nightmares.

The comorbidity of it all, my shuffling sickness and the underlining caustic conditions, were just too difficult to be ignored by Elise or Seane. I returned from their bathroom a drugged laced atrocity due to the crackling smoke I inhaled surreptitiously. As with all demented, altered states of speaking, the broken vernacular of a broken outsider uttering a dreadful language no longer served me well. In the beginning, I conversed with fragmented elegance whilst the tongue turned blue hues. Germinating the vegetable minds with boring thought poisons, I posited this or that notion of nothing in particular. But the mounting words I used to achieve this, to garner any semblance of murkiness in the minds of mice men, burst like billions of dying stars and their noxious gases, consequences and more consequences, seeped upon my waking world. My speaking abilities had devolved into slurred cadaverous things attempting to pass themselves off as meaningful verbiage breathing machines.

The phase in life when one's mind is no longer endowed with the capability to catch up to the thoughts spinning hysterically around in their head is unavoidable. It was difficult to remember those nights when Elise would saunter up to my bedroom door dressed in a dangling shirt and panties to quote Shakespeare as the liquor dribbled from the corner of her mouth. The evening's obtuse charm when she was near no longer lingered.

With Elise, I only wanted to be legitimately accepted for my indecency before the smoke cleared and I was no more. I wanted a moth-like mother-figure looking down on me as the doctors conveyed to her how bravely I suffered before the yawning sky swallowed me whole. The war within was too great for me, and the things I spoke of were just useless slang made to give drink to the extremely unacceptable.

Abhorrent echoes permeated my head, ringing louder with each passing pulse of blood recoiling. I never admitted to Elise or myself that I was dastardly, that I was unable to get close enough sympathetically to care which way the body fell. During my wayward adolescence, I made several attempts to access the part of my brain determining, figuring, and counting the seconds, the minutes, the hours, and days, but could not ascertain its hidden agenda. My thoughts turned to stone and my head dropped heavy.

It was not for lack of effort. Not because some grand fabricator in the sky had it out for me. It was the way things twisted in the worm barrel way of life I dauntlessly engulfed. My obstinance to not believe anything rang thunderous and fittingly. Standing from the green gangly couch Elise and Seane sat upon, I announced my departure, cartwheeled out the front door, and never again returned to Seane and Elise's ridiculous ruins.

The gifted sons and daughters of the great western nightmare are punished with infatuations for innocence and the nobility of savagery. To amuse the masses, we punish ourselves ceremoniously to ensure our very existence is fraught with weakness? That awful life-affirming ache in my side reminding me the heart is close by and so are the levers and pulleys waiting to constrict its beating.

Eye sockets sunken from days without sleep. Hands bruised and calloused from pounding them against the wall of unending shame. The quickening deletion of self while selling each breath, one after another, to street corner merchants lurking. Reflecting on life, there is a tendency to withhold much to save the last act of life, to allow a little room for the possible, even the impossible day, when the proverbial daylight overcomes darkness, when the horse is led back to the barn, when the shepherd has second thoughts and diverts his flock from the butcher's block.

A despondent man walking slowly down the street is not aware of my watching his every move with such delight because deep down his frown is my frown and his unavoidable fall is my fall, my unavoidable slip back into total absence. How many times have I uttered the willingness to alter the hysteria growing within? How many mornings have I reluctantly regurgitated the evening's drunken meal of dry throat dust and bat wing stew? And yet, I have become a homeless voice within a much larger mouth. When the sheltered self no longer believes a single word the outside mouth expresses, it will seek conversations with those lacking in character, in moral fibers.

I told this to Andre one day while sitting on the front porch of his new house. We spoke of optimism and the plight of the willfully obtuse. He laughed and said, "You need to reassure yourself that things were not going to get the least bit better and that if they did, like death coming to one sleeping, you would not even notice it encroaching."

How is this? Cannot those nearest to my voice hear the earnestness of my just reproach? Am I the only unfortunate bastard on this earth seeking an exodus from the decomposing physicality of being? Emancipation from this repulsive world's wobbly wants and nefarious needs to find the slightest autonomy, before the passing away time with its horrendous blue-sky bursting, does a body good.

I found myself staring into a darkened sky the night I left Seane and Elise. The moonlight punctured the large white clouds held high from the fears mankind emanates while ancient heroes buried under mountains forced their lost theologies upward and the scarecrow too had its day as the formidable crows flew away.

How to make sense of all this coming and going conscientiousness with its hampered legs dragging the past into ever novel steps toward tomorrow's unending torrent? A substantial state of seriousness has consumed my hours. I dragged my suitcase full of decomposing corpses from place to place like a dragon dragging its fire breathing face. The scent is driving the angry gods and their hideous dogs, littered across the built-up facades humanity fabricates, mad like famine. One must traipse the distance between seeing and being seen, a void as immeasurable as the boundless space between this life and no more. A factious space where impassioned words are the entry point into pages barren of walls and without windows to air out the mind-numbing fumes of eventuality.

I knew the time to be unreasonable was short. At least it appeared that way. I made too many bad memories in this town, and the people around me had had enough of my drunken antics. I was growing tired of having to explain myself and my actions to people I thought little of, people still walking on all fours in nuanced places studying my every movement. The crumbling relationships established in this town were now thin and brittle.

Occasionally, when the vanity of evening becomes still, my thoughts dolefully dawdle over that peculiar time in the presence of Elise and Seane. A wistful place where submerged minds enter forgetfulness as the daylight becomes too intense.

I need to remind myself that once I was at odds with the comfortless cosmos like an astute lunatic demanding life bend to his every profane petition.

The vulgar friendships established during formative years besiege, become haggard, then haunt with nostalgic charm the remainder of one's life. It is wise to make them count as little as possible. We, the insubordinate masses of centuries unraveling, envisioned and faltered, will devour ourselves on tables of our construction. A generation nourished from the udders of disintegration. Left to count aloud the rules and dictates of wobbly leaders, we face the conning insurgency of tomorrow. These wallowing days, when all solemn and sanctimonious, I quietly reflect on past individuals no longer present and become smaller and dangle alone like the last orange red leaf on autumn's frowning tree.

Our paths would never cross again. I left that town muddled and headed back east in a Greyhound bus to find a new hole to crawl into and froth for a while. I carry each person I have been or have known with me as I amble into surrounding walls of irrefutable regrets and can still hear, when a remote crack appears, the plague of mortifying laughter buried deep within.

Returning to the eastern half of the American landscape, a harrowing shock to the cold Cimmerian core caused much churning trepidation. Transported from the west on a bed of dying dreams, I returned to the place I left so tirelessly behind. The previous meat-and-potatoes path became ambiguous and difficult to follow. The homeward breadcrumbs placed were devoured by monstrous birds preying on sanity's mysterious meal. Those hideous creatures stole the forged foundations I relied upon to familiarize myself, to find my way.

I could not help suffering the calm demeanor of familiarity surrounding me as I existed the bus. This place was full of rabid canines roaming empty streets and ravenous men chasing after them. It was better to be familiar, but each and every day spent fighting off the trivial was soul suffocating to say the least.

Ravished by a rush of omitted memories, the nameless places and aesthetically diseased people existing in a tall tale told repeatedly to ensure myself a continued existence, I was nearly knocked from my feet while walking away from the Greyhound station. Not many hopes left. I trusted myself enough to know I would, once more, become bemused in this impotent place. My feet trudged upon the senseless ground. The cluttered mind becomes like a mirror unto itself when the sensitivity to novel situations becomes unbearable. The mask of audacity worn to ward off nonsensical features of life's petrifying grip, when reflected in the mirror's hallowed glow, laughs the laughter of a man tumbling from jagged cliffs toward the mocking grimace of the water's edge. The simplicity of life wants to be victorious, to be honored and commended for its remoteness in a world full of unreasonable realms, places of vast conformity where the masses go to die.

This town is smug. Listening to ludicrous sounds emanating from dwellings used to house politeness, I feigned awareness of self, became dementedly delirious, and nothing was remotely interesting nor was anything particularly abusive. Lecheries to rouse the devil's sympathy recoiled in this place. Villagers hung signs from commemorative houses to notify others of their obedience to a higher man-made law. They huddled under worn down worldly regrets to persevere in times of unraveling despair.

What did I believe before I left this place? How would I reacclimate without any intent to be civil? I remembered something Mark told me one night when we were both wanting more from life. He said, "the first time I felt seriously unimportant, when the darkness befriended me, I was lying in bed gazing blankly at the ceiling. I leapt from the bed's grace and ran absurdly through the house screaming and coughing up old bones. Not a single person in my family acknowledged the remorseless uproar billowing. Not one member stood in abhorrence nor turned in my direction. Instead, they stared at the television screen in muffled agony. As I slipped heroically into derangement, my living ancestors turned blueish as hushing noises slithered from their tangled grimaces. They despised me because I reminded them of what they were unwilling to acknowledge. What they knew, something all too familiar to my family's lineage, was upon me like a ruined shroud. You see, the men in my family were very acquainted with the haunting charm of eventual madness. My father too drifted in and out of his own suicidal serenade until the music ended and the rope became taut."

In light of Mark's actions, his being untethered by choice, it all made complete sense. To comprehend the manner in which he dauntlessly trudged, and the beaten path which led him to a cryptic place, the ambiguous and incomprehensible dwelling space within, I could find no equal among the saintly sane members of this trembling town. A little opening in the torn fabric of existence one enters to be consumed or suffo- cated slowly lay before me as I surveyed my new surroundings. A mixture of opaque emotions toward pending things with endings, cyclones of senseless contemplations swirling, and bewitching echoes spewing from a once optimistic persona garnered my reserved attention. Smoke rings permeated my memory of Mark's morphing face. Mark spoke in smoke circles. Self-prognostications for encroaching doom were birthed from his own insidious allegiance to generations of wheedled ancestors swinging from history's maniacal cord.

I endured that which lives behind the tiny openings before leaving this place. And upon my return, I donned the stupendous gown of shivering shame to cloak my wilting nether region. No longer was I merely existing. How could any semblance of sanity return from tiny worlds behind tiny holes without bringing back the foaming wretchedness buried below? How do I evoke the scent of tar boiling under the skin so as to arouse discontent in the minds of strangers? Demented ones with swollen eyes follow the falling water bustling along the gentle streets in this town. They tumble recklessly down impending storm drains to find sanctuary amongst the sewage.

The remembrance of Mark's ending dwells large on shoulders slumped and sobbing. I attempted to silence his persistent gasping voice calling, but the purging of cruel thoughts was a feeble endeavor. I needed extravagant silence to grow anew. Thoughtless gestures once flung onto crowds of familiar people seemed inappropriate and unnecessary. A crestfallen flock afraid to be doused in the putrid spectacle emitted from dank eyes, skunk eyes challenging and dangerous to well-breed noses, remained in this place like the fleeting echoes of a limited man asphyxiated. To be barren of intent and to lack all attainment ambitions was their *memento mori*. It was difficult to understand what Mark meant when we were both still breathing the same meticulous air, but there will be a reckoning, a time to disentangle all things before the final unraveling.

My voice remained tired as I wandered into the familiar place. The lips I spoke from, and the lips I constricted, were so full of mounting failures that I was not even aware of the time passing. I had not conversed with any of my fearful acquaintances since leaving, but one must attempt to rely upon familiar faces to give semblances of sanity in times of desperate need. Even though I despised them because they knew I lived a shelf life empty of reserves within consecrated walls built to prevent others from noticing my entrance into oblivion, all good options were limited and fleeting.

An old friend of mine named Stosh still resided in this old decadent place. He allowed me on numerous occasions to speak my mind plainly even when doing so would cause conflict amongst the hearing ones. I contacted Stosh to literally beg him for a place to rest and regroup. He generously allowed me to stay with him until I found some employment and a place to live. I slept in the room where he kept his boa constrictor inside of a large glass coffin at the foot of the bed. That night, I dreamt of being ceremonial snake food digested in honor of the great and wise reptilian-skin king.

I got up early the first morning back and walked to the nearest bar. The bar was a dim trifling place several miles away, but a man must walk a million miles to get nowhere and a million miles to get away from nowhere. When I entered the bar, I felt the apprehensive environment seeping from every murky corner and from every intoxicated pore. These feigning creatures smelt my sickness with their tender noses twitching, wickedly and without merit. I sat at the bar next to an aged man who coughed with each drag of his cigarette. He was boorishly loud. As the awkward inebriate spoke, enlivened words tumbled from his tongue like feathers of useless lofty banter floating across the blatant bar.

I despised the aging drunkard's feckless face. It was battle worn. The inpouring of abhorrence scratched at his soul. Contorting insides curdled from his spoiled milk-feed life. The unending futility of breathing wreaked havoc on his saloon style sermons. A stumbling state of defeat glazed over his eyes. Peering at this wobbly mess clarified the horrifying nausea encountered when staring into an abyss laden mirror.

Summer drenched the walls of this place. It covered golden temptations the morose men and women residing in the bar. After several strong drinks, I began thinking about the forthcoming, the imminent and the utter lack of enthusiasm I felt toward achievement, toward fully developed plans without plots or conclusions. The beginning of my new story takes place in a dark space on a wooden stool with gum stuck under the seat. Wafts of the detestable mingled with the scent of a diseased women's day-old breath. The unavoidable cluttered the room. Arbitrators of ghost stories, those who dread the coils of commitment and those who die perfectly alone gather together to drink away the inescapable privilege of being alive. Deadlocked does not seem so awful to the lonely frozen huddling here. The ignominy of humanity never loses sleep in here.

After six beers and a shot of vodka, I stumbled into a conversation with the babbling father of a twelve-year-old girl. The man's daughter had recently discovered the pleasantries of aesthetic endeavors. She was taking oil painting classes at her middle school for the nearly blemished and the hopelessly polluted. He pulled out a handful of pictures of her classroom art show from his denim coat pocket. His fat inebriated fingers smelt of sewage as he fumbled through the photographs. His speaking mouth reeked of undue glorification without a hint of representation as he belched out this and that achievement his mythical daughter attained. The alcohol made me delirious in disarming bitterness. Overcome with a sick petition to crush him with blunt force, I hesitated before drinking more. The over ripened father drunkardly engaged other unfortunate bar attendees, compelling them to comment on the merits of his daughter's portraits of milk white swans nestled on a blue pond.

"Aren't they incredible. She has only been painting for a month. Look at how realistic the swans appear and the way the water is blue. These are foundational achievements of a future art world sensation. What do you think?"

Most customers were kind in their applause and polite in their esteem. Not me. I was too intoxicated and too authentic to allow this kind of mockery to stand. Looking deeply into his pouting eyes so sickly in need of acknowledgment, so wanton in his emptiness, I said, "I am not an art historian nor critic, but I have to say, if she never touches another paint brush as long as she lives, it would bring back the light of the world, back from the impenetrable obscurity suffocating this worthless world unraveling.

"The mournfulness attained from glancing over these pictures laid before me can only be equaled to, or equated to, the dreary sensation gained from draping one's scrotum over the edge of a windowsill before slamming the window down with rigorous might and brute abandonment. The sensibility of physical pain is then distributed throughout the brain till blindness becomes a welcoming bedfellow. That is what I think."

It took him several minutes to process the lack of admiration I tossed into his lap. Reddening eyes quickly filled with the fury of disillusionment. Standing from his bar stool with fist raised toward my face, the unrewarded father announced his intent to thoroughly dehumanize my head with sheer brutality, followed by a continued barrage of battery until I struggled no more and dropped lifelessly to the floor. Could not blame him. But, he did ask.

Was this moment different from other occasions in life when words of reassurance evade the faltering ego, the mortuary of being? The daughter's pubescent achievements failed to provide the father with a glimpse of what always remained elusive to him; the steadfast security of time's devouring mouth gobbling up our eagerness and aspirations. The fumbling fingers of fate have their way with the lonely hopelessly afraid of tomorrow. The bartender intervened before a fight broke out.

Since I was not a regular at that godawful establishment and was unwilling to curb my words, regurgitating words full of the ugly insincerity all bar patrons drink to avoid, I was asked to leave and never return. I trudged reluctantly from the warmth of my bar stool and wistfully entered the blistering sunlight of midday drunkenness before an awkward grimace became my face and I turned to vomit poetically all over the front door.

No sense asking what mattered to me. No escaping the impurities coursing through my veins. It was cold for a change, and a chill of doubt wafted in my face. I headed back into the bar to announce some vindictive declaration toward those still inside. The lousy stock of frivolous fools still concealing their rote humanity from the midday malaise brought a slight smile to my face. They bathed in the smug lack of authentic feelings we smug humans present to defend the overwrought bulwark decaying inside of us all. But, before reentry, I noticed a police car pulling into the parking lot and decided to wander away like a good-natured slug covered in the scalding sting of salt.

Vague and frantic in my resolve to not hinder the deficiency of self-importance rattling inside my skull, I scuttled away with a pair of ragged claws dragging behind. Would there be a day when adversity's sullen regard no longer torments the homeless mind. A frigid cerebral existence is more catastrophic to minds unraveling. The mounting choirs of virulent dogs barking the blunders humanity enacts in general while lurid neighbors hiding in bushes grow boring, fattened, and secluded, is enough to make anyone thoroughly venomous. Could boldness ever truly be known to those defaulting on life? Certainty bequeaths uncertainty.

Tattered individuals trudging require the vanity of a hereafter to give pause to this insanity of self-importance. To fathom a misspent existence with acute veracity perverts the eyes of wintry folk. I meandered constantly, heaving and moaning exhaustively, over the uninvited physicality of death. Others with wrought iron fortified stomachs envision a past which has never existed in order to fathom some imminent guilt-lined thunderstorm and shame-infused monsoon they anticipate encountering in the crumbling distance. These blundering porcupine people scamper in vain for a more satisfying forecast. They grievously scour almanacs of banality written by the ghosts of antiquity.

May those unfortunates littering the streets of this place, those pint-sized people waiting patiently for supernatural parades of thinly disguised skeletons adorned in golden headdresses and glistening shoes made from the flesh of human weakness, abide by this absurdity no more. Instead of the merits of meekness, they eulogize earnest aspirations to be veraciously forbidden. Shivering simpletons paying homage to the new kingdom-to-come devour the flowery air with nonsense lungs trained to inhale things antithetical. Forgiveness is the lazy steward's foul-smelling bedfellow.

The needed alcoholic delights were dictating my thoughts. Their derelict-like charm would soon need to be rekindled. Such was my entrance into the second day back. The once familiar air was staggering and suffocating. A pneumatic epoch of dread filled my lungs. The sons of Noah filled my thoughts with apodictic visions of final floods. I went back to my room at Stosh's house and passed out on a bed of needles in honor of poor bastards wheedled and the young girls who paint realistic white swans on blue ponds for their drunken fathers.

Dust filled my dreams. Awakening's calm pleasantries did not last long. The pillow under my dull aching head was coated in the blue bile seeping from my mouth. I began to dread the uncomfortable certainty of walking upright. Intoxicated memories elude the mind of a sorrow filled man. To appreciate the greater importance of being uncivilized, I confronted the inevitable cowering face berated by another blackened morning mirror. I washed the salt from under my eyes. I did not question the senseless behavior of absurdities gathering at my feet, nor the guiding premise that to die without guilt was not a true death, but a resolve into the terror of not having lived or having lived without a moment of clarity to justify the heap of dreadfulness one assuredly becomes.

Moving from the floor to the window to smoke another in a series of lonely cigarettes, I noticed the sky twisting gray clouds into tube like tunnels of uneasiness. The encroaching humidity became unforgiving. It drove me to further my steps into the afternoon streets with a calculating fascination. To once again place my steps over the coarse ground where old blood was split to resurrect the vile inhabitants inhabiting these blacktopped urban streets. Once again, I had to find some employment, some means of subsistence to provide myself with an abundance of the maniacal. An unkempt decadence dangles just out of reach of the serious and sane servant, but I am neither as I trudge.

One requires the cool eloquence of the monetary to delve deeper in hollowed out corners. The dungeon dwellings of drug fueled strangers allow entrance for a price and a piece of your poison. A penance paid for being unlikable and unmanageable. The dungeon masters allow pasty pulsating figures to sit in their living areas drinking cheap red wine and smoking all manner of delirious substances for a considerate compensation. Substances sold to furiously drive conversations forward into an appreciation for messianic jazz are consumed by all in attendance. In impervious back rooms, the corrupt carnal acts men perpetuate on other men, tired men cubs longing to be recognized, are kept sealed off from the normality of gentler, kinder bears. A fee must be paid for frivolous backroom things.

So it was as it always is when the gestures of wanton women gather at the feet of devils donning sneers stolen from the tongues of lions. It took several hours before I got myself together and walked out the door. I was going to see an efficiency apartment on the far east side of town near the forgotten depreciating area.

It was a small single room, and it smelled like moldy dog food. Dead food left out for a long-gone canine friend. I found it acceptable and paid the first and last month's rent with the little money I had left. I decided to spend the first night heavily intoxicated whilst sitting naked on the empty linoleum flooring. It was cold like the steel on the wheels of an object moving aimlessly through aimless space. I spent most of the night talking drunkardly to myself, trying to rationalize the loneliness, and deciding whether or not to wander around the apartment building.

Not knowing whether my lack of forbearance might end in a situation unfavorable and ripe with the mysticism of finality, I pictured myself setting off for a noble war to calm the throbbing anxieties swarming my stomach. A bevy of men dressed in leather from head to toe, carrying knives sharpened on the sidewalk's cement and illuminated from the hanging street lights, stood by my side as the frothing rabid mouths of audacity marched toward my location. Hideous hordes of frightened bedwetters intent on plunging demented daggers into the shield of squalid flesh covering my chest. They lunge their pointy weapons with such furious acrimony. The dreadfully naked, those unwilling to falter, and those without the need to completely surrender, remained along the sidewalks in silence waiting for me to hand them a couple dollars to crawl back into the caves they came from.

I went out of my efficiency apartment and quickly found the sickness I was only conscious of whilst sleeping. Sloppy drunk waltzing slowly down the road, I held out my hand and waved tiny bills through the dangerous air in need of relief. Mercurial men ambulate along the streets in this place. Obnoxious women spend nights sloughing as the spectacle of life became too alarming to even look up. The exchange was made, and the monsters were free to roam again.

Crippling consequences pummeled my thoughts before clawing them to shreds as hit upon hit of inhaled insanity overcame all likeness of being brittle. Consequences, sweet consequences, were not something these roving street aberrations were unaware of as they stroked subtle gestures to condemn a demented social fabric, one tattered and torn from roaming hypocrisy. Unsightly grimaces reminiscent of the confused frowns trapped moths make when beholding the spider descending its web shrouded their facial features. The hopelessly captured unravel upon accepting the immense misfortune of becoming nourishment for another one of God's insidious creatures.

Not understanding how my formidable form was so unsuited for existence, the street horde was not the least bit impressed with my having gouged my eyes figuratively. They pirouetted before me all frayed and unbalanced. The sickened masses are furloughed to plagued sidewalks to consume large amounts of what hell coughs up. Shadow men barren of conscience covet things strictly prodigious to mainline into trampled veins. They wanted something meaty to dig their fangs into before the plundering and pillaging takes place.

As I sauntered along all drug addled, the forsaken faces I passed were either still and hidden like taboo tombs carved out of poached elephant tusks or loud in abomination with swelling sorrows draped around burdened necks. The more I came into contact with other human fatalities woolgathering their dolefulness, the more I learned how to hate myself with little effort. Time and effort are necessary when developing proper methods for assimilating self-destructive condemnations. Before attempting to refine the art of being willfully obtuse, before undermining all possible goodness in the fallen world, the nearly dead must first conjure a remote place in the brain to despise all prolonged bereavements for the innocent infant dying within. The death of innocence haunts us all, but it thoroughly embodies these broken bodies littering this place.

Nothing seemed real as I trudged through this place inebriated on kabbalistic sauce. How to not notice the deception of ambition in a world filled with apathetic trolls hiding under dauntless bridges linking the sane to the insane. The modern man's anhedonia wreaks havoc on the lives of those suffering from a tiny will. Caustic crustaceans waiting for something miraculous to come along and drag them from the oceanic floor. The depths of their despair grow exponentially deeper as daylight turns to evening's nightmares. A fortified fruitless place the likes of which their shivering arms could not begin to grasp has engulfed them. The scolding hot cauldron of civility cradles their sleeping souls. The thing sought most in the daily humdrum banality of leashed creatures escapes these diseased children who prefer the bitter sting of vulgarity over the mind-numbing touch of conformity.

I was resolute and lived my days with full abandonment. My face tilted toward the impenetrable sun awaiting its glow, waiting to have eyes scorched from sockets dim. My skin blistered and burnt to ash as the scolding winds of unfavorable aftermaths blew it toward an ever-present emptiness. I took note of the difference between what I was and what I knew I could never be as long as I assimilated disturbed sensibilities. The wobbling world requires its depleted children to surround themselves with the arbitrators of reason, those senile men dressed in robes and bursting halos. Such a worthless endeavor. Foolishly furnishing triumphant accolades for lives lived without sin. Walking upright canines and wayward down facing felines conning their way into the castles of forgotten kings and beheaded queens. Unlike these unfortunate bastards, I was not afraid of taking grim glances at yesterday's follies.

I choose not to be one of those treacherous citizens birthed in scented fields of frankincense and myrrh. I was not fearful of being unrecognizable. I proudly displayed my ever-growing contempt for everything glistening, mundane, and politely putrid. And like a well-worn mouth overlaid with the nausea of innocence, that boorish elixir of life flowing daunt-ingly from the child's unmade bed, I wiped away the crusty remains and trudged forward.

3.

In the horrible translucence of hindsight, I should have struck my evil queen dead in her tracks. The first time I laid eyes on her, I should have left her a wobbly blob of decaying rot for the worms to devour, but I was overwhelmed by the motion of her thighs as she approached me like a coiled python poised to devour its prey. Assaulting with hints of plagues to come. Striking out with fang-like gestures shredding my stoic face. Snarling while her ruinous aroma turned my blackened blood to sot. Dusty wafts of blood black dust gathered around my hardened neck when I met my dear Fortuna.

I should have known I was going to relish all those vanquishing depravities dangling from hell's unhinged grasp as Fortuna's two blue dungeon eyes caved and sucked all the polluted air from my lungs. She was nothing like death's bantering. She was the nefarious tide of locusts festering and feasting on sneering emotions parched.

My weakest parts exuviated doubts about Fortuna's necessity. They expressed the devilish desire to be offered up to Fortuna in an ecclesiastical moment of sheer agony followed by the dripping forth of gold flakes and spiders morbidly boiled. Her lips deliberately parted as she told me her name was Fortuna. My lips diminished and withered. Her hand reached out to greet me as if from some gruesome grave for disdainful drudges to drag me down into the expressionless below, leaving only my dribbling head to rest above ground. Left there to be calibrated, humiliated and prodded over by throngs of well-meaning well-wishers analyzing Fortuna as she stood before my bodyless head, motionless and heedless.

Having experienced the sheer bitterness of Fortuna's sting, I would never again be burdened by even the slightest sliver of decency. Things cluttering my thoughts with trudging and unraveling became mute. To live eternally and probe the deviant gestures became the new mantra. Murky roaming rings of dismay fell like mad children at her feet. Fortuna flung false expectations from her sturdy sides whilst cavorting with the whirling swirling plight of mankind. She would, forever more, ride roughshod over the barrenness my blackened hole of a heart space generated. Not even the slightest touch of matrimonial bliss envisaged would be evermore lacking in light of Fortuna's blistering existence.

The brusque local bar in which we met became eerily quiet while the reeking heavens fell upon our encumbered shoulders. The slivering sorrows my Fortuna and I gathered while apart, while living morbidly deceased, were freed. Released, they swaggered over those futile expectations existence inhabits when the lights are turned down and sounds of rushing nothingness slumbers the intoxicated to sleep. Our repugnant breath coated each other's palpitating presence and purged unmentionable trivialities from time's hallowed grasp as the liquor flowed quicker. We stared quizzically at each other before allowing ourselves the awful pleasure of greeting each other's hidden devil.

Fortuna. What kind of nightmarish creator would bequeath a soul to something so void of simple serenity and so full of volcanic acrimony? I slightly remember asking Fortuna if I might buy her a drink, but I cannot be sure. Was it me asking Fortuna for her company or was it the raucous sounds, those distressing notes composed by countless ravens encircling, echoing from distant places within my chest heaving? The maniacal music of soaring isolation seeped slowly from my empty rib cage space where the God of Adam had previously removed a balmy bone to fashion my dear Fortuna. She agreed to a drink and we sat at a small table at the back of the bar.

I ordered a bottle of reasonably cheap red wine. The Dionysian deliriums would mask the deplorable scents emanating, the dolorous odor of desperation, and the suffocating air of sulfur surrounding us. Once that sulfuric scent gets under the skin, its impossible to wash from one's blank being. Scouring the dead flesh from my frail frame would lose all its cryptic charm after that evening's delights transpired.

We sat across from each other without speaking as I poured the red wine. My thoughts were raging in every direction, and my heart was beating so fast I thought my chest was going to leap across the table and pin her to the ground. Fortuna held the glass to her mouth, took a slow deep sip, and swirled the wine around in her tight little mouth. She leaned into the table. Her lips swelled in succor. I was going to be Fortuna's final prey, the last to be devoured.

Fortuna's lips came within inches of my hysterical face drooping. I smelt the lingering remnants of aberrant cocaine smoke lapping against dear Fortuna's quizzical grin. The scent of regrettable death haunted her taunting appearance. She took a long drag from her cigarette and placed the glass of wine on the table underneath her mouth. Fortuna allowed several slow drips to descend from the cautious corners of her mouth and mingle with the cigarette smoke. Liquid soot acquired from trudging aimlessly through burnt fields of unmistakable horrors, the sheer abomination of being above the godless ground, encircled our lonesome table. Fortuna was a well-spring of brooding blood squeezed from the insides of things diseased and lacking in wonder. The immensely pure milk of forthcoming follies burst from Fortuna's innards as cruel barefooted seraphs danced atop rustic needles gathered around to give drink to Fortuna's fountain of erotic and grotesque sensibilities.

Fortuna placed her mournful mouth next to my ear and, with a trifling whisper-like voice, whispered, "I want your hideous cock to rape me over and over till my insides reek of the seething sadness suffocating this world. Suffering the festering humiliation of one savagely raped by choice is the released beast roaming. Dig yourself, your profound pale cock, deep inside my afflicted bellyful of unborn blisters. Cum so mercilessly hard that it scorches my tepid insides like a sorcerous lava flow. Curdle my shriveled egg yolks into putrid sacs of diseased bereavements so I can encounter ethereal death once more before the grave grabs hold. So I can declare my life a neglected ulcer, a pointless incurable ulcer deserving of the self-hatred I choose to define myself."

I felt my cock stiffen as Fortuna spoke, then it maddeningly burst into sickly smithereens. An oozing mess of slurry courage ran down the side of my leg. A fluttering noise of birds being swallowed by a brutal tornado blotted out the pathetic cries for yesterdays rattling around in my drunken head. Who is this worm witch? With so few well uttered words, Fortuna stole and shackled the very essence of my wilting will to live and brought it ever so near the precipice before begging me to leap toward the darkened cliffs of shamefulness below.

"You want me to fucking rape you?"

Without a second to lose, she lunged toward me and screamed, "I want you to fucking tear me to pieces. I want you to fucking rape me, smack me, kick me, punch my mouth till my lips split open and my teeth fall out. I want you to slice my arms up with dull razors and throw sulfuric salts into the wounds, then dowse me in gasoline and incinerate what remains. After being vengefully consumed by the nauseating fervor, I want you to ponderously piss on the living flames till the seared crumbs falling from my burnt frame become like pieces of charcoaled beef to nourishes the lowest of insects nestling. And then, I want your cock to morph into a large black vulture to pick at the charcoaled pieces until your cock belly is stuffed, then flies off toward murky mountains in search of a funereal cave to defecate my digested body-meal."

The idea of seeing my cock metamorphosize into the mother of all vultures was something unfriendly to my senses, but the senses can be foolish errand boys. There was a figurative line I would not cross, and this was definitely not that line.

Begrudgingly, my lungs breathed in the vomit-tinged bar aroma. Swallowing the noxious pollutants spewed from the inebriated mouths of customers swaddled in fear was amazingly propitious. As if a smokestack sourced from their timid souls was pumping ashy gray loads of regret, disappoint-ments for not being anything, and shamefulness for having done anything, directly into the frowning barroom bonanza. The billowing remorse these dreary drunkards coughed up slips directly down the throats of the thankful sinners sharing this place. Hampered lungs hastily reject the formidable plumage of acidic saloon scents swirling before crawling out the mouth to hide in some corner of some dimly lit place.

Barely can I characterize the frothing decadency Fortuna embodied upon releasing such a full-throated deluge of homespun absurdities. I was but a laughing stranger birthed on a beach of rotting carcasses in her presence. Fortuna was the heroic hellion wanting to truly relish the shamefulness of being mortal before passing out in a cloudy coffin of regret. Fortuna arose from her chair. She hovered around my seated stature at first before slowly rocking her thighs back and forth in front of my crumbling face. Fortuna knew I was the sickened and repulsed one who would nourish her regrettable appetite.

Fortuna held the half-empty glass of wine in one hand while placing the other hand under her shirt. She made tiny circular motions around her nipples with fumbling fingers.

Closer and closer her slithering body swayed. I knelt down on the filthy floor, then prostrated myself divinely to honor the approaching allure of Fortuna's fateful alms. Fortuna took her hand from underneath her shirt, poured another full glass of wine, gulped it down in one tremendous swallow, then placed her cold hands on my enervated face.

"Get up and let me take you somewhere you are unlikely to ever return."

I hurried to my feet, erect like one about to be crucified to the shadows, then followed her out the back door and into her car. As soon as she closed her door, she dug her right hand deep into my pants and squeezed my cock so hard it turned red bluish purple, grew three tiny horns, and became filled with the abhorrent pain of maturity. I begged Fortuna to rip it off my body. She smiled like the devil herself and, after a slight laugh, said, "In due time."

Fortuna started the car with my cock still swelling in her hand and drove off in a furious rage. There was nothing I wanted more than to have a Fortuna shaped shovel split my head open wide, then tear the brain from the cord and bury me in a hot wet display of utter vandalism. Nothing mattered more to me than to give Fortuna my death. Nothing made sense to me. I was a bursting thing without the slightest ambition to become quelled, to become a porcupine like member of a putrid and indulgent society. I was Fortuna's new sunken skull.

Fortuna drove down winding streets, traveling alongside rows of rotting buildings boarded up and covered in bog moss. She breathed deliberately, and promptly turned her head toward my dumbfounded form each time the car halted under stop lights frowning. Fortuna began laughing menacingly as she tugged my cock harder and harder as she drove faster. It was impossible for me to even maneuver around in the car seat to give her a better angle from which to rip the skin-sheath from my fruitless cock.

I did not dare to even utter. My mouth was like a hot clammy tomb full of deceased words. Rotting imbecilic words like wandering zombies churned in my mouth hole, awaiting their unsightly resurrection. To be torn and reborn into the land of the living frog men, those sulfur men reluctant to die a fitting death, would be an exuberant display of self-immolation to laud my dear Fortuna. The deceptive welcoming she bestowed whilst drunkenly contorting at the bar was only a vague hint of her intentional madness. The sheer volume of perilous henchmen, those lackluster men laboring under Fortuna's every word, invoking diabolic defenses against over ripened onslaughts perpetuated by grainy moralists, those frisky pugilant bedwetters, was clearly staggering as they cleared the way for a future without reason.

Fortuna slammed down hard on the brakes as the car twisted and skidded to a smoldering stop. She stuck her head out the window and yelled disingenuously into the crystalline sky, "The worst is yet to come for the best. The towering and forlorn children will persevere until the last days of mythical men walking on all fours."

I could not help drifting out the window, studying the sidewalks traveling alongside our trudging vehicle. They were tattered and littered with the remains of feigned and forgotten faces. The malignant debris from history's charred remains accompanied them. As we drove over a litter of stray animals and stray people sinking into the tar nothingness, I closed my eyes and pretended I was blind.

Many times in this storied life, tasteless modernity is confronted by the unbearable likeness of what a singular sensibility has granted to some and denied to most. Fitful fate can be a severely whorish beast which never doubts whose cock to cover with blistering sores. Ridged red sores burning. Suffering sensations pulsating. The ungodly sounds of yellow puss dripping. Fortuna's womanly ways were never acknowledged, never hungered for, by the lonely broken shadows, the ones with scar-covered arms, scar-covered mouths, sacs of scars lugged about, burdening their formative shoulders.

If it were not for all those wretched and deplorable fortune tellers with their historic blindness, and those hedonistic horoscope hunters searching for a spongy fix from today with their crystal ball death traps starred into whilst the abyss stares back, we would forever remain transfixed in the mere ever-present unfulfilled. As the hunger for a savage death overtook me, my Fortuna, basking in her remote longings, gathered my thoughts as we slipped quietly toward oblivion's all to charming engagement.

There is a means to achieve the very least possible things in life, to enrage the vilified senses, especially the senses stimulated by filthy things hiding in tiny holes. The lumbering car ride was excruciatingly long. The night-slick roads we traveled upon were worn out and loathsome.

An objectionable odor began emanating from within Fortuna's car. I first noticed the scent, one reminiscent of ruined cheese left outside and covered with the bodies of pillaged cats, plundered walruses, and several daunting bowel movements heaved from the assholes of mankind's sinister twins, benevolence and sensibleness, the moment I entered her car. The soothing pungent bouquet of finality. A poignant agonizing aroma radiating from some mysterious source made my throat close periodically in horrific delight. The depraved fragrance knew its malodorous air would engulf my lungs, and vomit would become my lap's companion. I tried to sneakily roll down the window so as not to startle Fortuna. She appeared easily alarmed by any sudden movements as the car sauntered along.

Other than the dry yanking of Fortuna's arm tugging my inflamed member, the occasional flipping of her head out the side window, then down toward my lap to investigate the palpitated purple cock head swelling, all else was hushed. I clumsily reached for the knob to open the window and reduce the amount of nausea swirling around in the consuming reticence of the car's interior, but the handle was bent down and would not budge. I hoped her cigarette smoke would kill the worst elements of the aroma, but it was not to be. The putrid quality of the scent grew on me like dumpster moss. The stench thickened and tore ferociously at my nasal passages until they became resigned in a benign quietus.

What in the land of things nightmarish was making such a wretched stench? Fortuna looked at me and noticed the gangly green quality my face was taking on and asked, "Do you smell that, that sickening fishy-musky-death-like smell?

"Yes!"

"Good," shrieked my dear Fortuna as she slammed down on the breaks, bringing the car to a thunderous halt. "It is the blood-soaked mess of unadulterated rage foaming between my legs. I recently stuffed my bloody femininity with a couple gobs of infected cotton swabs swiped from my doctor's office dumpster three days ago. They're molding into place between my moldy lips, all vulgar and tainted, awaiting your time-honored mouth and pristine teeth to exorcise the diseased rages from my mourning drenched fertility, my seething little piggy."

There is a need to separate mere fact from mere fiction during one of these watershed moments. Trudging forward into another bestialized and self-abused predicament, a place of overwhelmingly bastardized dysphoria, I did, at that very moment, exhumed by the frenetic shock of pure lucidity, bury my revolting mask of a face into Fortuna's lap. Fortuna calmly rolled her hips forward while leaning back in the car seat. I took an enormous life-affirming inhalation of my ogre's pungency, leaned back, then exhaled vomitus bursts of everything dead in the world.

As if the shuttered sky cracked wide, a calamitous cauldron of blackened bile, cheap red wine, and several silos brimming with soaring shame and elevated remorse filled my embittered throat before exiting my mouth volcanically. Bursts of searing acidic mess tumbled repetitively into Fortuna's lap. An avocado monster of fragility was birthed from my belly. The horror was so invigorating. I slowly lifted my heavily labored head and glanced up at Fortuna smiling with inordinate delight. A bellyful of pernicious stomach rubble rested on her shivering lap. The despondent fauna fragrance of decomposing corpses recently dug up by grave robbers, who then violated the two-day old corpses in necrophiliac splendor before looting them of all their sanctimonious wealth and deadened values, permeated the car's interior.

Where were the divinity days promised? Days to be covenanted. As the mountains trembled and ingloriously crumbled. As the boiling lifeless seas reluctantly receded in utter defeat before the ever-diverging ocean swells? What has happened to those gallant intrepid men, those lionhearted herds roaming over lofty virulent landscapes, places where mephitic death is hidden away, tucked away, into the familiar places where commonwealth noses and their gregariously concocted diseases run waterfall rampant?

What has become of their unforeseen reasoning? Has it been touched yet by the sheer eagerness of knowing how morbid things were going to get before the boundless flood of time washed all mankind's base instincts down the shithole of existence? The smile on Fortuna's face as the vomitus mess seeped into her pants and surrounded her swelling lady parts was a flutter with all the certainty I would ever necessitate.

The inevitability of fathoming fate's scruples proclamation, that there is absolutely nothing to this ape-man evolution after the prickly fingers of daybreak death arrive at dilapidated doorsteps, was a warm friendly reminder to needlessly violate everything nailed down.

Fortuna laughed hysterically as she started the car and proceeded without wiping a single bead of regurgitate gore from her soddened lap. The car became a mythical place, a moving away from place, emphatically ripe with carnal anticipations, at least it was for me. I wondered whimsically about the layout of Fortuna's living space. What it was or where it was? Was it a depleted apartment building or an echoing cavern carved out of some jagged mountain range along the edge of some deserted town? The fascination of knowing the other's demented dwelling place is a sickening delight used by many to distinguish their own crippling and noxious domicile from their neighbor's enviously prying eye hole of a home.

The westernized mind relishes in thoughts of starving pilgrims walking the new earth, the deserted earth, free of pious volcanoes, without a single drop of fresh water to drink or useless coins to toss into allegorical wishing wells. Snake oil forefathers, coiled around humanity's growing reluctance to starve off the privileged breeders of dismay, surveyed the untouched lands and found them bountiful and in need of gluttony plagues. The majestic footsteps of wandering migrants littered with memories of egalitarian landscapes were eradicated to make room for more poisonous skyscrapers and polluted soda fountains. A poor populace sermon preached the virtues of wholeness and uprightness before hastily resolving into a mire of betwixted human complacency.

Fortuna is the breath exhaled from that hopeless experiment of horsewhipping the self into conformity. For allowing such indulgences as peace and tranquility to run amok, Fortuna became blistered. When she was a child, the villagers surrounded Fortuna with lustrous swords and blinding words dampened to extinguish all tiny gestures of good-will. They encircled her in shoddy expectations, but Fortuna arose fluttering above the duplicity below, above everyone's substandard convictions. Fortuna never spoke an utterance the first seven years of her life for fear the words she was being taught would woefully constrict in her unfledged mouth and plunder her nightmares with horrible notions of rosiness and ravishment and rectification.

As Fortuna grew, her arms and legs woefully withered from lack of lightheartedness. She took on the appearance of a wingless cherub abandoned to the ungrateful ground. When she learned to stumble, the feathers of adolescent fragility, those tattered plumes of self-mastery, fell from her flourishing facade. In time, my dear Fortuna's steps became, in and of themselves, an endless series of calculated attempts at self-mockery in a world that values the progress of pride.

No one ever told Fortuna she was enchanting or mattered or was something created by an all seeing all powerful cosmic breath. Fortuna was the embodiment of indomitable dread. Awe-inspiring trepidations were internalized by the morning child. Abused and tossed aside by the trolls of decorum, Fortuna was raised to savor and adore the fleshing eating culture. The child's brutality was taught by devouring greed machines broadcasting venerated cartoon creatures on television deadfalls made to mar the core of youthful imagination. As shadowy adolescence turned into well-adjusted adult tribulations, the absurd gloom of an all too human nature rang victorious.

The calamitous streets Fortuna and I drove aimlessly down that rustic evening were serpentine. We traveled alongside the winding sidewalks and a continuum of empty aspirations and broken promises superimposed on the trampled bodies of rumbling circus freak types rummaging in dreary rain-soaked dreams. The surrounding building facades have been replaced with large, extra-ordinary sized tombstones declaring the same worn-down mantra.

"Humility is its own reward."

The immensity of the misleading message crowded out my consciousness. My forehead tilted to one side as the falling rain saturated the car's windows. Fortuna had a delightful grip on me. It was the grip I needed to be gripped by. The maniacal twisting hurricane grip of self-destruction will never be real enough to wipe clean the accumulated burdens I incorporate into my bemoaning being, but it is a sweltering start. Fortuna must have intrinsically known that I was a different daybreak entity, different from the frightened lot of anesthetized villagers she once clung to, once knew thoroughly.

Fortuna was birthed specifically to inhale the nauseating bouquet of heartbreak commingling with lost generations, upon lost generations of objectionable bed sheets stained in righteous urination and bucket loads of blackened civic bile piled up outside and left to proliferate. The sickening stench creates anew every morning's malaise along these godforsaken streets. The gentle repose of the sidewalk's fleeting coddles repugnant philosophical remnants of immorality seething.

The unchosen ones inhabiting this once thriving dominion of mice now hunker down around bleak barrel's burning for a source of light. A welcoming chimera fluttered through my wondering mind again and again as if a stream of sterilized water was building within me. The ebb, the life defying ebb, was halted leaving only the flow, the deafening flow of misery seeping from under the very bedrock of brittle being, under the malicious mantle of envious skin, under the ever-dying inner child raised on junk food commercials and cartoon balloon dogs.

The obligatory mettle obtained from Fortuna's presence was like a warm syringe loaded with Morpheus's evil elixir. A dead panacea for a dead population. She must have known that I am not human after all, but merely the burnt carcass of another thousand-year-old tree left to decay upright until its trunk goes barren and the colorless leaves gathering on the cold ground, those twisting reminders of genuine innocence, rot in autumn's intangible glow reminding fellow travelers of death's hauntingly emasculating grin.

The radio suddenly died. Fortuna turned the car into an unlit parking lot of what appeared to be an abandoned industrial building complex covered in the markings of another time, an epoch of drudgery when mankind hobbled in front of machines belching out massive amounts of plastics and bullets and shared ambiguity. Fortuna tossed quick shifting glances about as she surveyed the dim surroundings like a feral beast cornered and riddled, fearing the unknown atrocities to come. After several seconds of barbarous silence, Fortuna finally spoke, "Get out of the car, and put your cock back in your pants until I tell you to pull it out again, understand?"

I hesitated before answering. The appropriate reply eluded me. I wanted to remain buried under Fortuna's unspeakable mercy. Having already given myself to her venereal yet wanton ways, I simply questioned, "And when will that be?"

She gave my cock a sudden jerk, then shoved it back into my pants while staring directly into my sheepish eyes. I zipped up my pants and exited the car fully aware I was nothing in the ever-growing nothingness all around me. It was marvelous.

Fortuna exited her side of the car. She walked to the front of the car, motioning for me to follow. As we entered the fawning landscape, the ground beneath our feet was unusually soft for that time of year. The gravely ground smelt less like the wholesome earth and more like fulsome sewage sprayed periodically in this particular location to suffocate any bushy-tailed remnants.

"You are probably pondering why I brought you here? You are probably dying to know what vindictive thoughts of vitiated vengeance are running around in my rancid skull mind as your throttled cock is now reeling in pain and your tarnished limps weakened from licentious anticipation, like an miasmic blister on your thigh you cannot wait to drain just to watch as the impure puss drips down your impure leg," Fortuna said in a half laughing voice.

I was not in the least bit concerned with where we were going as much as I was longing to find out what dreadful things would be there waiting to tantalize tormented nerve endings. To be held down forcibly in the moldy mildewed morning before the sun's gaudy glow scorches things darkly hidden was a pleasantry unraveling for me alone. Eclipsing wayward cockcrows with true daybreak grit, instead of those comically vain sensations experienced upon awakening, enlightens those brutal bastards of banality. No longer heroically reaching for existence anew only to find your tormented blood spilt and spread out over rustic westernized streets. Opaque as the tender flower of misery, my blessed Fortuna floats above, dangling the glistening blades of demise in her hands firmly.

"I hope you understand that I am fully at your command, my dear rancorous Fortuna. I have never met a tarnished queen with such low-grade resilience. I humbly wither before your crippling demarcations used to ward off the cleverness of disentangled dogs from all those pointless pigmented desires of the old flesh. I will remain your steadfast and submissive evolving mess my insurmountable Fortuna. You mournfully materialized before my narrow world of perceptions blurred like a reluctant warrior hawk hoovering over its reluctant prey, golden and pathetic, waiting for its turn, its nature, to extinguish all life in due time." With a sullen quip, Fortuna turned her lips inward, biting down on a scar under her bottom lip she received as a young girl working the swollen streets. A disobedient memento left by an unhappy customer she apparently sucked on a little too long.

As I surveyed the slippery scenery of this most morose of situations I found myself in, I began to recognize myself in everything covered in the sickening stench of a thousand lifeless bodies buried beneath the skin of my feet, those capriciously asleep ones who grew shovels for hands out of sheer necessity. They audaciously adjusted to history's broken promises and the unquenchable and reverent need to be underground. These were mankind's real boisterous behemoths. Timeworn souls fashioned from dying stars. Their folkloric remains are culturally forgotten and collectively transfigured into a meal for worms and fairy tales alike.

"What is this place?" I asked.

"This is the diseased place," said Fortuna. "The grotesque location where I was fiercely festered by roaming rapists, solemn burglars, and licentious individuals teaching the forbidden knowledge of veiled humility and what it means to be amongst the living dreadful. Those lurking patiently will deny my ethereal charm swiftly as they crawl back into their demented holes. Those keen to the unflattering world around us will stand triumphant at my side. I was transported here in a car similar to the one which brought you. It was an unforeseen vehicle. A mystifying means for moving obscurities from place to place without the passengers, those frigid folks on the inside, from ever having to notice the in between places as they pass. Harbored on all sides from the outside remoteness, they travel at alarming rates toward another dying tomorrow daydream.

"When I was brought here, though, the ground was already dried and the bodies were all fresh and only buried a foot beneath. They were yet meals for the footprints walking over them. The penetrating winds traveling across the somber facades decomposing in this place gives most stragglers a frightful forewarning. The final arrival is at hand.

"Nothing here is known to the world of outside minds festering alone in gray closets. Those menacing outsiders never truly venture near these forbidden catacombs, but instead, they choose to be like the dolefully entangled, those insidious fools biding themselves to the bones of immaculate deceptions, bound forever to immobility. This is the place where the howling herds and forsaken storytellers find time to contemplate their impending doom. I hope you find it as unpleasant as I found it when it found me. It will all be yours once I am dust-born wind."

Stumbling through Fortuna's smoldering footsteps, it occurred to me to ask her how she wanted this thing to go down. I was gullible. Would she take me under her feral falcon wings, steamrolled and trounced in Fortuna's vilifying nest, some dingy bedroom cavern I presumed, then converted into something resentfully unreal, yet something seething in sinister sensibilities like a sacred lump of cancer in the throat of fate's evil cough.

I could not begin to even engage in suggestive thoughts regarding Fortuna's naked body writhing. To perceive of her barren womanly hole covered in wiggly worms and haunted verses as she straddled my core, ripping out polluted thoughts from her disquieting hairdo, drawing forth the monstrous root beasts hiding in her brain, bludgeoned all prior thoughts of fading civility and dashing gentlemanly demeanors. I wanted to wake up withering inside her. I wanted to make sure Fortuna was not just another yellowing human skin sack filled with metal shards and broken glass.

Fortuna motioned for me to follow as she turned toward the entrance of a faraway two-story house with boarded up windows and no apparent electricity. The shrubs surrounding the house were a derelict brown. Dead little pine cones littered the grass. The grass was coated in a black oily substance. A field of blackened slick bile regurgitated from the barbarous bellies of forgotten plague people residing nearby. A seeping sulfuric scent saturated the surrounding grounds, drawing forth the infamous worms. I approached Fortuna slowly as if my feet were dragging bags of old dinosaur bones behind to delay the inevitable. Fortuna lugged the weight of the rueful situation we were about to enter, one as serious as an entire world coughing up caskets, coughing up children's nightmares, over her sharp shoulders as she trudged forth.

The motion of Fortuna's hands wildly waving were utterly debilitating. She reached out and quickly grabbed my arm. Fortuna firmly pulled me to her side. Together, we became timorously tangled like rolled barbed wire entwined with the hair of a donkey's mane.

The windless air encircling us was deranged with the unexpected pleasure of solitude. There was a tiny hint of apprehension welling up from within, but not nearly the tidal wave of wafting pestilence lurking about in the foreshadowing darkness. Angling for the right narrative to understand shrouded obviousness, I no longer feigned interest in hunting for the diseased delicacies feed to feeble herds. Fortuna smiled and coughed up some more blood. It softly dripped from the corner of her mouth in the most authentic manner, like winds pulsating across the desert unafraid of the dry coarse sands beneath.

"I am going to make you into something inhumanely grandiose, something to be destroyed by the mischief of vermin till you egregiously fathom the sincere nature of my cruel affliction," declared my dear Fortuna. "I want our nuptials, our profane union, your utter growing remoteness forged to the obscene silhouette of my essentials, to be divinity's unbecoming. You will never reap anything laudable from this sinister escapade. The last thing you will see is the sliverly glimpse of a giant damning eye peeking out from behind impending storm clouds billowing.

"There will be no eternal goodness glorified nor will there be any menacing lullaby like resolutions to scrutinize. Your distaste for this ever-present place, as you drift unforeseen across the dying days, over and over again in muted indignation, will not cease. I do not want to replace your imaginary boldness with heaps of golden dreams. I want to drill holes in it, then fill it with boiled rat parts mixed with a thousand horrendous hypocritical lips sown shut to insure they no longer speak of righteous legitimacy nor noble deceit."

I was overtly brimming with nausea. We made our way to the side door of the house. Rotting rubbish left by the previous proprietor was strewn across the shifting yard. There was a pungent pile of decomposing dog corpses neatly stacked up alongside the side of the house as if waiting to be tossed on some proverbial funeral pyre.

There was no lock on the door, nor was there a doorknob. You merely pushed and the door would open wide. As I entered, a mammoth waft of the foulest smelling odor again struck me. The sadistic stench of a ruinous skunk severed in half savagely battered my pale pinata face.

Fortuna enjoyed the aromatic discomfort her guest was greeted with upon entering her depleting dwellings, her dead space unraveling. She grinned the grin of antipathy commingling with delightfulness as if she was witnessing the woeful and whimsical obsessions life so generously grants to its broken children.

A corridor laid before me. Its walls were the color of charred flesh wilting. They twisted sardonically in and out of my diminishing field of vision, then morphed irrationally as they traversed the receding distance. We traveled steadily into an unmoved serpentine-like tunnel to somewhere unfamiliar. Somewhere so damning and remote even luscious words were terrified to enter for fear they would become murderously deconstructed. Nothing glistening ever returns from places of such absolute emptiness. Someone recently spray painted the walls with nonsense, mostly descriptive words announcing the coming of the end or the beginning of nothing new or something regarding the fabric of life being ravished and torn asunder by flocks of passing ravens with razor sharp talons.

Was it the illogical I was encountering, consuming, like some vague notion of shared civility I once knew so well? The revered barrenness of being systematically hides from down-turned eyes and nailed-down tongues which no longer speak of existence decorously. A fleeting conception of self without the clutter of being relevant overwhelms the contempora-neous crowds gathering around historic shrines to worship themselves. I could not make up my mind. Was I feeling anything? Was the wine, the poisonous Grecian brew, wearing off? The demise of self-awareness, like a vindictive whore on a winter morn, took hold of my bleak shoulders, then drew them down as I became anew in my servitude to Fortuna's ill begotten will.

As I followed Fortuna down the corridor and up a flight of stairs, she turned to me and said, "I want your fingers inside my bleeding cunt. I want your fingers to dig and dig and find a new spot to dig further until you reach the very foundation of my spoiled core and inscribe your scathing signature there so I will forever bare your mark, your riddle. Will you do that for me? Will you finger your way through the blood and mud and contamination?"

I could only nod in the affirmative. Fortuna nodded in reassurance. There would be a formless foundation from which my dear Fortuna flowed, but the walls housing her unhallowed bedrock would be enscrolled with many savory names, many tempting curses, and many severed ears nailed down tight to hear the approaching doom Fortuna generously offered. A new book of death would be required. The names of the tormented and brutalized, the bedlam ones with lifeless nomenclatures the old book tossed aside once bloated with noble signatures deserving malodorous redemption, would be scorched into Fortuna's leathery ledger. The flock of Fortuna's blistering brood will bare her name rustically etched onto the backs of fluttering heads. The afflicted children of Fortuna will be known to hobbled villagers as they wander cities spreading disease, insanity, and the godless act of contrition.

Could I be the only living creature trudging along? Who else fathoms the hateful blessings Fortuna offers to the dying world of dying words? The urge to shout aloud came over me. I quietly quivered before screeching, "I can hardly wait to see your face when I pull it out. The back of my throat is coated in lice eggs. May I begin drawing blood from my arm? If it pleases you my dear Fortuna, I can also recite a sorcerous verse or two from some old, weathered manuscript. One day, when the moon is full and a circle made of cow entrails to dance within appears at my feet, the haunted realization of a woman with ghostly demands will devour the burdening urge to destroy myself."

Fortuna shook her head as if to give some affirmation. My prickly presentation of self was too soon for her liking. Fortuna had eons of damaging details to drape me in like lizard skin, thick and abrasive to others, but bearable if you have no other line of defense.

What was within these curious walls? What little things would be found here? Something unusual had gone missing for century upon century and was hidden within these walls waiting for prying eyes. Some portal to a towery perdition, one imparted to man by the gods of antiquity, built on the encumbered backs of withering herds, infected men and mean women, remained undisturbed for centuries behind these vacillating walls. The brooding offspring of these historical builders of absurdity morphed into industrious hammers and arcane chisels. The golden yolk of earthly compassion dried before their faulting awareness, before their groveling inhibitions were poured forth to gild the gardens of mankind's growing inhumanity.

Fortuna led me toward the ever-present life affirming nothingness. She dragged me drunkenly along a treacherous series of pathways leading to dimly lit rooms. One particular dimly-lit room was full of decomposing dog corpses brought in from the outside pile by the previous owner apparently to be used as a source of fuel, a dog kindling of sorts, to ignite the warm reassurances inhabitants gathered in dread require to ward off the unnatural elements of time and rain.

I would soon know. I would, very soon, never again regret staring at another horrific image of myself in the mirror. Never again would I want for the frigid ghosts of eternal death to visit like sympathetic bedfellows stealing the warm linens, then soiling the pristine sheets.

We entered a small room. The walls were plastered in lifeless wallpaper peeling. Tiny pictures of mangy dogs without leashes hung all over the room's interior. There must have been twenty or so pictures of those hideously unleashed beasts. There was a tiny wooden chair in the back corner of the room. Fortuna signaled for me to be seated. It was then I realized nothing. I was a catacomb of despair made from the lies of a thousand dying memories unraveling.

Fortuna began speaking in a lethargic voice unlike anything she previously presented. "You must understand, I am not a source of light in the darkness for you. In fact, I am that which gives life to the darkness. The true nature of my blasphemous being will be known to you. You will then have to make a decision as to how far you are willing to go before you cower and run hysterically backwards into your sleepy singularity. It has been lifetimes in the making. I have spent lifetimes watching, observing, as the tiny men wandered around the world searching for each other's breath. Insignificant misanthropes pursuing that which gives steadfastness to their meager flicker of an existence.

"They will always rise and fall in the dullest of moments, those spilt seconds between the insignificant years piled upon the unnecessary years of banality. For mere boredom has cursed them, and they are its maidservants. To envenom your brittle being back into existence, I will harm you so deeply, you will beg me to cut off your arms and legs and dispose of your flesh, but I will not give in to your lusterless voice."

As Fortuna spoke, her legs shuffled and she grew a reptilian tail. I inwardly noticed the tail's presence protruding from her backside well before I outwardly noticed it. Fortuna turned richly red like Chianti wine was being birthed from her veins, drenching her clothing. Fortuna slowly removed her dripping attire, piece by piece, until she demonically bemoaned and danced in a Dionysian swirling hysteria. The room was still. Not even the air was allowed to enter our conversation.

My mouth timidly opened as I declared, "I was dreading this day. I dreaded knowing I would someday realize this disease was a lie. My bitingly benign mask of a mouth was a vacuum. The vacant words I casually hurled about from demented tongue snappings have returned as ceremonial daggers sent for my godless demise. The caustic blades of a misappropriated youth are now embedded into my throat. I would, without a hint of reservation, graciously regurgitate at your feet, my Fortuna, if only the bloated urge to be sincere had ever crossed my mind. When the distinct pain begins to dissect my will to live, when my eyes, shriveled and burnt, fall from their sockets like sand from a shattered hourglass, it will be enough to say I have done enough with my life."

Fortuna surveyed the room with hauntingly blank eyes. And with a polished pining deluge of regrets formed over a millennium of waddling sorrows, she motioned for me to remain seated in the tiny wooden chair in the back corner of the room. The chair was draped in a red velvet cloth. When approaching Fortuna, the legless legs swell and twitch in acceptance of the pale coming forth of absurdities overflowing. It was better to remain seated before her unbecoming. Fortuna gently slumbers that which is still dreadfully awake.

I sat down on the wooden chair. Fortuna knelt before me exquisitely. She fastened the binders attached to the chair to each of my ankles tightly. I noticed all four legs of the chair were bolted to the floor so as to give the impression of immobility. Fortuna stood and walked quietly behind me. She snatched up my faltering arms and quickly bound them at the wrists with a piece of rusty barbed wire.

I was untenable, dangerously complete, barbed wire bound and in the control of a dreary worm woman. My dear Fortuna finally reduced me to a glued viewer awaiting the wretched spectacle unraveling. An oblong puzzle piece made for no puzzle, my guttural determinations to be a nebulous walking wound were densely present. Fortuna finally seized the fortitude I so foolishly prided myself on, before devouring the entire lonesome sunset of sanctimony sinking within me.

Fortuna spoke not a single word the entire time she bound me to the chair. Instead, she made impish whispering-like noises one might hear when placing their ear upon the tombs of recently departed bygone monstrosities. Fortuna glaringly grimaced as she took stock of the situation. A vague hint of laughter gluttoned her mouth.

My pounding pulse shuddered, became unsteady, then skipped in fear of living another moment without the blessings of Fortuna's formidable finality. My sweltering skin recoiled and uncoiled repetitively as Fortuna swayed and breathed in and out. A fluttering of ocular delights captured the harsh stillness of the room. Fully undressed Fortuna stood before me like a mountain of otherworldly invocations. With ginger hair hanging down over bare shoulders like fiery rivers, like volcanic avalanches of molten lava flowing, she was fiendishly magnificent. The salacious deeds atrocious creatures commit upon their brethren poured from the back of Fortuna's skull cracked wide open like the tarnished vastness unraveling.

Fortuna's battered chest caved like the shoreline buckling under the ocean's devouring ebb, dragging away the salty remains of history's flow. The boiling water no longer quenched Fortuna's thirst for naive knowledge, unrequited despondency, nor the continuation of other worm men and women living hopelessly in their gutters, trudging through life with hollowed out cheek bones and tongues nailed down to immobile jaw frames. Fortuna's arms were like vigorous tentacles slashing. They were reminiscent of dynamic under-water structures covered in old moss. Fortuna flung them about the room probing for more pure air to consume and pollute. Fortuna's legs became two taunt and twisting pillars of salt as she stepped several feet back from where I was seated in drowning dog urgency.

It was then things became what they were destined to become. Fortuna appeared aporetic as she stood before a square wooden table four feet off the ground and made blackened by the surrounding bleakness in the room. In all four corners of the room appeared, out of nowhere, like the mumbling mist over an autumn moorland, four tiny figures, four decipherers. They were only about four feet tall at best and were draped in beaded burlap fabric as if shrouded in itchiness. The cerement sacks did not appear to be fastened to the tiny decipherers. The wicked material apparently clung to the futility of their fleshy coverings.

The decipherer materializing to the east of where Fortuna was standing, then approached me as if floating on a blanket of dead air. Infinitesimal billows of silent winds formed underneath its hideous drapings and carried the tiny decipherer to a halt within inches of my face. The decipherer removed a roll of barbed wire from its underneath and began fastening it around my forehead. I began bleeding profusely. The sadistic decipherer tugged tighter until it could be tightened no more.

The decipherer quickly receded toward its corner of the room awaiting the hushed approval of its ill-begotten benefactor. A gusher of gluttony then erupted under Fortuna's feet. Fortuna was raised up, levitated over the table, then halted and slowly rested upon it. Her hands and feet were hurriedly scooped up by the four decipherers.

Procured from the deep underneath, the four decipherers held out glowing red spikes in one hand and mallets made from gold in their other. The spikes and hammers were rested atop each of Fortuna's hands and feet as if to secure them down, to restrain the deafening Fortuna beast about to be. Neither searing threats of bitterness nor the obligations of gaudy gold could hold down the mounting mountain of Fortuna unfurrowed. Did these tainted decipherers not know Fortuna was the renewed and modernized fattened calf?

The decipherer to the west of Fortuna pulled a tiny copper cup from underneath its underneath and raised it toward Fortuna's blemished femininity. Fortuna's whole gawping women hole became somewhat blurred and began to rumble. A thunderous booming Tibetan horn sound engulfed the inside of everything as a flurry of feral locusts poured out from within my dear Fortuna's pink folded flower. Dilating throngs of razor tongued locusts scurried and scampered over all things inside the room. Everything except me and my dear Fortuna. We were spared from these devouring living things, spared to die alone in fear years from now.

After the torrent of nasty bugs desecrating, a stream of spoiled porridge-like sewage began dripping from Fortuna's still strikingly wide-open woman hole. The decipherer with the copper cup caught the horrid brew until its cup runneth over. It raised the rancid smelling liquid over its head as Fortuna screamed toward the barrenness behind the ceiling, "Drink from it, all of you. It is my crud."

To this command, the tiny decipherer with his tiny copper cup floated toward each of the abating decipherers obeying Fortuna. The decipherer poured several drops onto the tops of each burlap bag shrouded decipherer, then over its own before placing the copper cup on the ground beneath Fortuna's feet. The copper cup was swallowed up and returned again to the unsightly underworld from which it came.

The decipherer from the north corner of the room approached the base of Fortuna. The decipherer removed a brass bucket from underneath its nether region, then raised it toward Fortuna's rectum brooding hole. Like the blistering blisters of fate bursting, my wicked Fortuna released the most noxious bile of rodent boiled infantile brains, autocratically aged yeast, the burdens of a trivial youth, and a cup of poisoned water with a hint of morning glory from her bemoaning breech.

Again, mighty Fortuna screamed demonstratively toward the still barren ceiling, "Take and eat. This is the lifeless mud from my infuriated asshole which I have defecated in honor of your humdrum horrors. May no fruit be born from this world again."

The decipherer carried the bewitching cauldron of Fortuna's internal sewage, made external, to each awaiting decipherer. The northern decipherer poured a teeny amount of Jezebel drudge upon the tops of the three opposing decipherers before dumping the remaining excrement mélange upon itself. The emptied pail was then placed on the ground beneath Fortuna's head. The foul-smelling decipherer returned to its northern corner of the room. And, like the copper cup containing the vagina spewing locust brew, the brass bucket was swallowed up by the infuriated ground and taken down to the sacred place where the profane is tucked away.

I remember thinking about places where old dogs go to die. Questioning myself in the face of mundane madness, I could not help unraveling. What was meant by this ridiculous spectacle of reverse revelations, this enchanting nonsense wreaking havoc on my diminishing sense of uncertainty? The sirenic need of anticipated answers spewing from the hallow mouths of dying old kings was no more. The same quizzical instincts which once reported back to me regarding bountiful things no longer bore the same grand facades and flowery veils to hide behind. Before the belfry brain became polluted with predictable goals, faulty achievements and glorious wreath baring apparitions toting the keys to things needled, the earth's surface was already busy rotating remarkably around another dying star.

It was not always dark in these wandering woods. It was never truly well-lit either. If beguiling scapegoats grovel before the socially acceptable troth long enough and with much gusto, they will be remembered by those who dine on insignificance. Each boring morning dies another slow death waiting to be diagnosed.

Fortuna then became the enraged mess. The four decipherers approached Fortuna from each of their isolated places in the room. They floated like puzzle pieces toward her swollen hands and florid feet before coming to a profound halt. They each faced Fortuna. They each whispered in the other's direction.

Fortuna raised her reddened head from the table and stared directly at me, directly through me. As the bittersweet blood began to pool under her eye holes, Fortuna howled at the tiny decipherers, "Rape me, you horrible little creatures. Tear me limb from useless limb as you savagely desecrate and enrage the new endless vessel. You timid flock. You labored souls roaming countless terrains with heads tilted down like brutish bedfellows abandoning their beds terribly unmade.

"You blighted fools crossing the ocean's swell in search of novel emptiness to consume. To purge yourselves of forgotten reveries, you shrivel under the awful curse of daybreak. Surviving off the fat of a dying land, you mask yourselves in monkey skins and huddle in above ground shrines celebrating your pensive civility. Your death is forthcoming. I am merely the coming before, the one who walks the shifting messianic streets in search of locusts to devour. Obey and be made unwholesome again."

The four decipherers hurriedly grew twelve-inch swords unsheathed from their underneaths and began plunging Fortuna. Plundering her pillaged parts over and over. Cramming shameful swords into Fortuna's sanctified sides, into her vulgar eye sockets, her ear tunnels deafening, her maddening mother-maker of a hole, into every ounce of Fortuna's pale withering flesh. The decipherers' swords were masterfully cruel. Each insignificant cell of the bloody awful mess, the newly formed Fortuna corpse, was utterly ravaged. The decipherers began to chant, "All hail the dying whore. Her death reunites us with punishment's true aim, that grand designer of the huddling masses."

Fortuna never made a sound. She never shrieked in horror, never attempted to remove or tumble the spikes and mallets resting upon her appendages. Fortuna remained silent like a tongueless lamb before the butcher's block.

When the four decipherers finished ravishing the once erect Fortuna, they calmly withdrew their sweltering swords, sheathed them underneath and returned to their respective places in the room. The room became insanely scorching as a radiating glow formed inside the underneath places of the decipherers. A gratifying luminosity finally burst forth from the decipherers' underneaths. A brilliant barrage of historic dust, Egyptian sandstorms, and woeful wishes coughed up by dried insignificant wells, swallowed the room's interior. Blinding bubbles of fiery things frolicked. Orgies of the most hideous hues suffocated all life. The decipherers, no longer of any real value, decorated themselves with nothingness and became like rust colored soot dropped from above. The four decipherers then vanished into that slippery distance forgotten in time.

The taunt barbed wire turned to ash and dropped from my head. The binders on my hands and feet turned into a slick tar-like substance, then dripped to the floor beneath. I stood erect on my hind legs for the very first time. I took my first step toward the newly formed Fortuna mess fragmented on the table.

As time inevitably catches up with us all, I feared, in some not so remote past, I might have played some compelling part in the table's design and construction. How could I begin to describe the mess before me? My Fortuna. My golden age. My dream of becoming burdened, becoming like the righteous weight choking the necks of the soon to be departed. No more would this be. I slithered inside myself, then stood tepidly beside my Fortuna mess in wonder.

The wild dark yonder then tore itself wide in half. The insidious excrement of divine nothingness flowed down from its mammoth bowels, flooding my head with meandering words, deceitful words spoken by verbal derelicts who read insatiably. A simple hushed voice coming from behind Fortuna's dead eyes attempted to enunciate something from Fortuna's flaccid lips no longer twitching. The gentle hush within Fortuna's tarnished head quickly turned into a tempest of tormenting colloquies. Fallen Fortuna then christened me with an ugly utterance formed from the damned hands of damned things.

"You are my birth. My loins are your loins. My filth is your filth, and it will remain with you as you become the second one of me, the second one to dine at the elongated table with frog men from all four corners of the globe.

"They will shelter you and enunciate you to the waking world. They will make mounds atop the grandest of mountain ranges in honor of your becoming, my prudent child. My tender little flicker. They will adorn themselves with the decadent weight of your being. Sorrows will hang from their necks as a reminder of your having arrived second. Go now and never return. This hidden place will be no more once you leave. Once you enter the anew. Fear not, my birthed thing, you will assuredly perish one day and, on that day every thousand years or so, the living will gather to burn things in your memory," the hushed utterance announced.

A feeling of pestilence grew inside my chest. A mad calling to heave heroically from the table's side confronted me. Fortuna went blank and swayed before me no more. Madness swiveled. The pathway toward insincerity pulsed. The poached sky above bemoaned and exhaled the heavenly fire Fortuna gathered from below.

I reached for the door to the outside place, opened it, then ran as fast as a deer from the arrow's owner. The car headlights were on. I assumed the keys were still in the ignition where Fortuna had left them fearing for her return. Lullabies of blurs intoxicated my vision. Doubt tugged on my shoulders. The dead hands of pipe dreams pulled me downward. Hopeless hysterics pummeled my petrified steps. I trudged desperately toward the awaiting car running. The pulsating chariot appeared ready to return me to the land of my forefathers, relics of the past who became like pallbearers, conduits for caskets traveling from gilded gates to their final resting places.

For what seemed like a split second, I was at the car's side door, entered its interior, then slammed on the gas pedal so hard my foot nearly punctured the floorboard. Squalls of soured perspiration flowed from my forehead and mixed with some blood dripping from somewhere. With sanguine fluid filling my eyes, I raced from the final place of my newly formed Fortuna corpse and fled down the nearest road. Faster and faster away. The gas pedal pressed firmly down. The rubber tires, infuriated with gravity's pull, squealed, screeched, and squawked like a thousand talons were tearing at the road below.

Within minutes, I was far from the sight of that final place. Its rotting image no longer resided in the rear-view mirror. It was then I noticed the first police car. The rest is undoubtedly known. The drunken car chase with the furious blue men. The drunken jail cell smells. The cold damp place from which I began this story.

Epilogue

They stand around waiting for the morning meal to be delivered by the grossly overweight guard who seems perplexed every time I request moldy bread with my meat, but in here, this gloomy gray holding place, you are told what to eat and when to eat it. I have three more doleful days in this box before the outside world welcomes me back into its bosom, bound over to the convictions of my neighbors who, with their own demons to fight, decided to make room. A reintegrated madness survives and thrives after many bitter moons of corrective rehabilitation of the caged sort. Soon, the ebbing beast will again roam the shifting world.

Three more days until the air my lungs have been coughing up ceases. The rustic dust shed from the sorrows of incarcerated men, wafting through stale cages, will no longer inhabit my breath. No more will the inside air sour air sacks with moral pestilence, courageous contaminates, and other corruptible devises made to leave the chest heaving. In time, this caustic substance populates spaces left blank and unkempt. The imprisoned mind, littered and tattered from the meanderings going on inside this place, revolts with exalted, yet meaningless, demands on the outside place. A sordid insurrection against the groundwork of judgments littered with reverential tombstones.

And soon, they will become anguished. Their mounting anger and destructive self-judgments, condemning themselves to a future of bloody awful messes, will seep back into society's malaise. They will simmer no more. A deluge of diseased creatures will overflow in a tidal frothing fashion drowning out the serene days. Beneath the surface of things pristine, the ill-begotten spend their days and nights boiling. Surviving off this toxic billowing brew of fleeting sanity, revolving doubts, and the unfettered desire to be dastardly, the days inside become minutes, then become slow seconds as the importance of time disappears into a tiny string of obscurities for counting minds to fawn over.

The deplorable space inside covets the outside world expanding. To exist without the flaunted morbidity of infected outsiders covering themselves in fig leaves and hanging signs regarding some new morality, some new demands to either perish or punish, around vaulted heads like good little bastards, is required of the soon to be released. They utter gaudy-imbued gibberish while attempting to find gentle reprieves from previous obligations to be authentic. Generations of vindictive snakes will flourish on westernized streets. The naked ones, those insignificant sheepherders with tiny feet and heads battered in disbelief, will be forbidden from even copulating on burning boulevards for fear their unruly offspring may come upon them and demand justice for their indecency.

Nomadic reflections shelter me from the all too familiar places inside where the rabid dogs thrive and the faithless surveyors of time go to die. The hours spent in here were not wasted. The story of a man wantonly disregarding roads paved and lined with phosphorus slithers along unrequited. Choosing the unflattering path of the least diseased is a dangerous endeavor, but worth every broken footstep taken.

The lingering shadows have quietly grown over me like the slick film left on the shower room floor after the gang's good washing. The blatant images of well feed herds roaming lush green pastures, and the mindful routes taken by the cynically irredeemable, lack all the seriousness of a faded philosophy once used to fuel the great disease in here. No more time for dinning on such fruitless things.

I lived these unspeakable things, maniacal mazes traveled down fast before the next blur occurred. Before the depleted will of the fleeting masses resurfaced. Before the face of the new homeless was agreed upon. Before the new guardians of envy assured us of their decency. Watch and wonder as the new keepers of civility tote such warm regards for citizens daring to speak of dire disruptions, towering disappointments, and the delicate art of becoming nothing by not having anything for the sake of sanity. Did I ever feel the guiltless hand of judgment? Was I ever truly allowed a respite from the engulfing fog of memories tainted with confusion and childhood?

And what about the many mistaken transgressions? What is to be made of those thoughtless actions taken, then haphazardly tossed aside. Nothing gained. The will requires a sacrifice to prove its worth. To test its fictional fate. To test the whore of a liar buried under beguiled feet. To make a defenseless case for something not precisely known.

A fluttering mind comprehends the totality of the mess. The misinformed ideas launched in youth by a hurried culture return to shatter the inaccessible calm of the infantile ego. The boundless rivers of joy, slashed by the shorelines thick tongue, flow no more in lands where certainty thrives unabated.

Timid things held nearest to souring souls are not optimal for engagements with the infinitely unpleasant unraveling. Pollute yourself with unsound things. Dangerous words regaling self-migration away from goal driven lunacies contain the basic ingredients for a life free of societal diseases. Shuffling through demented days not knowing whether tomorrow was a golden messenger sent to guide, a breath worth breathing takes on an abysmal hue. A rescuing vision committed to coddling the weathered steps of wandering sufferers with pillows of plenty fails time and again as lullaby time inevitably takes over.

It does not seem like I am existing in the present. After so long in here, it just does not seem like the present. The dead past with its army of rats gnawing and ransacking and tearing holes into my story of self-flagellation have taken over inside this place.

The outside place is where tomorrow's tormenting smiles reside. A place free of futuristic diseases and populations permeated with petulance. Free from guards with long dog faces and nefarious intentions. Authority's moralistic mutts linger outside the door to tomorrow, safeguarding its majesty from those no longer walking upright. Have I stared long enough into that sky? The squared off square of sky distorted from the several thick layers of incarcerated glass one looks out to remember they were disengaged before the cell doors began slamming?

In so many ways, I tried to wishfully agree with myself. To instruct myself to change the cosmos into something utterly vindictive from the very start. To banish the meek throat from which I speak. To replace the feeble fingers used for fumbling under tables divine. To erase the places dawdled over and the disappointments dispensed. No longer desiring to be suffo-cated slowly. No longer swallowing the sewage and polluting myself again and again. The faceless nights and never-ending siren songs wallowing across the sickening frowns in here have dismantled the flowery fiend I use to be. The weeks victimized the days with more uncertainty, more numbers in a ceaseless series of spent calendars crossed out and forgotten. Soured years dumped into yesterday's trash bin. One should avoid the trash of time before regrettably becoming its moat.

In three more days, I will become a new member of the glistening tribe who honors time well served. The others inside here, the miserable herds and the chosen few, will have to devour each other upon my departure for there is no hope left in here for them, nothing in this place to relish, to long for before one is long gone from here. They are the children of a formless cage, a race of caged birds without tongues to whistle with as they flock no more.

The unmoved creator, the one who once watched over us, that gigantic being before the before who raised the trees and moved the first movers has stopped being concerned with the disgusting mess. A characterless creation unraveling. We are left to suffer unseen, alone and unafraid of father's wipe cracking as we trudge through the valley of our own discontent.

The End

Printed in Great Britain
by Amazon